D1489010

Stories of Saint Nicholas

New York Classics
Frank Bergmann, *Series Editor*

Santa Claus, or St. Nicholas,
by Robert Walker Weir, West Point, 1837.
Gift of Mr. George A. Zabriski, 1951.
Courtesy of the New-York Historical Society.

STORIES OF SAINT NICHOLAS

· · ·

James Kirke Paulding

With a Foreword by
Frank Bergmann

SYRACUSE UNIVERSITY PRESS

Foreword copyright © 1995 by Syracuse University Press
Syracuse, New York 13244-5160
All Rights Reserved

First Syracuse University Press Edition 1995
95 96 97 98 99 00   1 2 3 4 5 6

This book is published with the assistance of a grant from the John
Ben Snow Foundation.

The paper used in this publication meets the minimum requirements
of American National Standard for Information Sciences—
Permanence of Paper for Printed Library Materials, ANSI Z39.48-
1984.∞™

Library of Congress Cataloging-in-Publication Data
Paulding, James Kirke, 1778–1860.
    {Book of Saint Nicholas. Selections}
    Stories of Saint Nicholas / James Kirke Paulding : with a
foreword by Frank Bergmann.
        p.   cm. —(New York classics)
    Selection of stories originally published in: Book of Saint
Nicholas. New York : Harper and Brothers, 1836.
    ISBN 0-8156-0325-8 (alk. paper)
    1. Nicholas, Saint, Bp. of Myra—Fiction.   2. Dutch
Americans—New York (State)—Social life and customs—Fiction.
I. Title.   II. Series.
PS2527.B66   1995
813'.3—dc20   95-8396

Manufactured in the United States of America

Contents

Foreword

James Kirke Paulding (1778–1860) is dimly remembered today as secretary of the navy under President Van Buren and as one of the Knickerbocker writers associated with Washington Irving. Irving used Dutch material effectively in *A History of New York,* "Rip Van Winkle," and "The Legend of Sleepy Hollow," but scholars agree that Paulding is his superior in sketching life in what was the New Netherlands. Unlike Irving, he was himself of Dutch background and therefore had a deeper interest in the history of the Dutch settlements from Long Island to Albany.

Some of Paulding's best Dutch-American work was collected in *The Book of St. Nicholas* (1836). Not all of the stories in that book have to do with St. Nicholas; the present volume reprints only those that do. Paulding was inspired to write them by Irving's whimsical references to the good saint in *A History of New York* (1809) and, most likely, by the popular success of Clement Moore's poem "A Visit from St. Nicholas" (1822). Paulding goes against the historical record by changing the fourth-century bishop Nikolaos of Myra in Asia Minor into a sixteenth-century baker from Amsterdam whose story is told by Nicholas Aegidius Oudenarde, a fictitious minister in New Amsterdam, the future New York City. Throughout, Paulding emphasizes the Dutch nature of St. Nicholas and the old Dutch-American customs and values. Some of the stories have an anti-Catholic touch, which may be explained by the Protestant fatherland's struggle for independence from Catholic Spain in the sixteenth century; in fact, Paulding makes specific reference to the ironhearted Spanish king Philip II and his stern general, the Duke of Alba. Paulding's anti-British and pro-Dutch attitudes may be traced to the American Revolution and more specifically to the War of 1812: he was a fervent American patriot, and the Netherlands had greatly aided the American colonies in achieving their independence.

Paulding tells his tales very deliberately and digressively, lacing them with social criticism. Younger children may have trouble following "The

Revenge of St. Nicholas," "The Legend of St. Nicholas," and "The Author's Advertisement," all of which are for older readers; they will, however, greatly enjoy "The Origin of the Baker's Dozen," "Claas Schlaschenschlinger," and, for the most part, "The Ride of St. Nicholas on Newyear's Eve."

٭

A note on the text: Though the first four stories appeared separately in magazines between 1831 and 1833, all of the selections in the present volume are reprinted from Paulding's *Collected Works,* vol. 14 (New York: Harper and Brothers, 1836). Except for obvious errors, the original spelling—such as "holydays" for "holidays"—has been preserved. The stories are sprinkled with Dutch and occasionally German phrases, most of which are explained or translated by Paulding right where they occur; they certainly add more flavor than confusion.

If you want to know more about Paulding, the following are useful books: Larry J. Reynolds, *James Kirke Paulding* (Boston: Twayne, 1984); Ralph M. Aderman, ed., *The Letters of James Kirke Paulding* (Madison: Univ. of Wisconsin Press, 1962); Amos L. Herold, *James Kirke Paulding: Versatile American* (New York: Columbia Univ. Press, 1926). The most thorough historical study of the St. Nicholas tradition in Europe is written in German, by Karl Meisen, but there is an informative and highly readable account of Santa Claus in America: Charles W. Jones, "Knickerbocker Santa Claus," in *The New-York Historical Society Quarterly* 38, no. 4 (Oct. 1954): 356–83. Robert W. Weir's 1837 painting *Santa Claus, or St. Nicholas,* serving as frontispiece of the present reprint, is discussed in R. W. G. Vail, "Santa Claus Visits the Hudson," in *The New-York Historical Society Quarterly* 35, no. 4 (Oct. 1951): 336–43. Vail makes a point of saying that "Saint Nick is a real Dutch saint and not the fat old fellow whom you will see in Macy's or ringing a bell on the street corner at holiday time, both of whom are descended from Thomas Nast's Santa Claus of 1890."

Goeden Hemel! I must not forget to thank Karen Orr and Tim Wong for retyping these tales. May the good saint forgive me for taking so long to introduce his stories, and may he richly reward all those who read or listen to them.

Utica College of Syracuse University   *Frank Bergmann*
Utica, New York
April 1994

Stories of Saint Nicholas

THE

Author's Advertisement,

*Which Is Earnestly Recommended to the Attentive
Perusal of the Judicious Reader*

You will please to understand, gentle reader, that
being a true descendant of the adventurous Holland-
ers who first discovered the renowned island of Man-
hattan—which is every day becoming more and more
worth its weight in paper money—I have all my life
been a sincere and fervent follower of the right reverend and jolly St. Nicholas, the only tutelary of this
mighty state. I have never, on any proper occasion,
omitted doing honour to his memory by keeping his
birthday with all due observances, and paying him
my respectful devoirs on Christmas and Newyear's
eve.

From my youth upward I have been always care-
ful to hang up my stocking in the chimney corner,

on both these memorable anniversaries; and this I hope I may say without any unbecoming ebullition of vanity, that on no occasion did I ever fail to receive glorious remembrances of his favour and countenance, always saving two exceptions. Once when the good saint signified his displeasure at my tearing up a Dutch almanac, and again on occasion of my going to a Presbyterian meeting house with a certain little Dutch damsel, by filling my stockings with snow balls, instead of savoury oily cookies.

Saving these manifestations of his displeasure, I can safely boast of having been always a special favourite of the good St. Nicholas, who hath ever shown a singular kindness and suavity towards me in all seasons of my life, wherein he hath at divers times and seasons of sore perplexity, more than once vouchsafed to appear to me in dreams and visions, always giving me sage advice and goodly admonition. The which never failed of being of great service to me in my progress through life, seeing I was not only his namesake, but always reverently honoured his name to the best of my poor abilities.

From my youth upward I have, moreover, been accustomed to call upon him in time of need; and this I will say for him, that he always came promptly whenever he was within hearing. I will not detain the expectant reader with the relation of these special instances, touching the years of my juvenility, but straightway proceed to that which is material to my present purpose.

The reader will please to comprehend that after I had, with the labour and research of many years, completed the tales which I now with an humble deference offer to his acceptance, I was all at once struck dumb with the unparalleled difficulty of finding a name for my work, seeing that every title appertinent to such divertisements hath been applied over and over again, long and merry agone. Now, as before intimated to the judicious reader, whenever I am in sore perplexity of mind, as not unfrequently happens to such as (as it were) cudgel their brains for the benefit of their fellow-creatures—I say, when thus beleaguered, I always shut my eyes, lean back in my chair, which is furnished with a goodly stuffed back and arms, and grope for that which I require in the profound depths of abstraction.

It was thus I comported myself on this trying occasion, when, lo! and behold! I incontinently fell asleep, as it were, in the midst of my cogitations, and while I was fervently praying to the goodhearted St. Nicholas to inspire me with a proper and significant name for this my mental offspring. I cannot

with certainty say how long I had remained in the
bonds of abstraction, before I was favoured with the
appearance of a vision which, at first sight, I knew to
be that of the excellent St. Nicholas, who scorns to
follow the pestilent fashions of modern times, but
ever appears in the ancient dress of the old patriarchs
of Holland. And here I will describe the good saint,
that peradventure all those to whom he may, in time
to come, vouchsafe his presence, may know him at
first sight, even as they know the father that begot
them.

He is a right fat, jolly, roistering little fellow—
if I may make bold to call him so familiarly—and
had I not known him of old for a veritable saint, I
might, of a truth, have taken him, on this occasion,
for little better than a sinner. He was dressed in a
snuff-coloured coat of goodly conceited dimensions,
having broad skirts, cuffs mighty to behold, and but-
tons about the size of a moderate Newyear cooky.
His waistcoat and breeches, of which he had a proper
number, were of the same cloth and colour; his hose
of gray worsted; his shoes high-quartered, even up to
the instep, ornamented with a pair of silver buckles,
exceedingly bright; his hat was of a low crown and
right broad brim, cocked up on one side; and in the
buttonholes of his coat was ensconced a long delft

pipe, almost as black as ebony. His visage was the picture of good-humoured benevolence; and by these marks I knew him as well as I know the nose on my own face.

The good saint, being always in a hurry on errands of good fellowship, and especially about the time of the holydays of Paas and Pinxster, and being withal a person of little ceremony, addressed me without delay and with much frankness, which was all exceedingly proper, as we were such old friends. He spoke to me in Dutch, which is now a learned language, understood only by erudite scholars.

"What aileth thee, my Godson Nicholas?" quoth he.

I was about to say I was in sore perplexity concerning the matter aforesaid, when he courteously interrupted me, saying,

"Be quiet, I know it, and therefore there is no special occasion for thee to tell me. Thou shalt call thy work THE BOOK OF ST. NICHOLAS, in honour of thy *patroon;* and here are the materials of my biography, which I charge thee, on pain of empty pockets from this time forward, to dilate and adorn in such a manner as that, foreseeing, as I do, thy work will go down to the latest posterity, it may do honour to my name, and rescue it from that obscurity in which it hath been enveloped through the crying ignorance of past generations, who have been seduced into a veneration for St. George, St. Dennis, St. David, and other doughty dragon-slaying saints, who were little better than roistering bullies. Moreover, I charge thee, as thou valuest my blessing and protection, to dedicate thy work unto the worthy and respectable societies of St. Nicholas in this my stronghold in the New World. Thou mightst, perhaps, as well have left out that prank of mine at the carousing of old Baltus, but verily it matters not. Let the truth be told."

Saying this, he handed me a roll of ancient vellum, containing, as I afterwards found, the particulars which, in conformity with his solemn command, I have dilated into the only veritable biography of my patron saint which hath ever been given to the world. The one hitherto received as orthodox is, according to the declaration of the saint himself, little better than a collection of legends, written under the express inspection of the old lady of Babylon.

I reverently received the precious deposit, and faithfully promised obedience to his commands; whereupon the good St. Nicholas, puffing in my face a whiff of tobacco smoke more fragrant than all the spices of the East, blessed me, and departed in haste,

to be present at a wedding in Communipaw. Hereupon I awoke, and should have thought all that had
passed but a dream, arising out of the distempered
state of my mind, had I not held in my hand the
identical roll of vellum, presented in the manner just
related. On examination, it proved to contain the
matter which is incorporated in the first story of this
collection under the title of "The Legend of St. Nicholas," not only in due obedience to his command,
but in order that henceforward no one may pretend
ignorance concerning this illustrious and benevolent
saint, seeing they have now a biography under his
own hand.

Thus much have I deemed it proper to preface to
the reader, as some excuse for the freedom of having
honoured my poor fictions with the title of *The Book
of St. Nicholas,* which might otherwise have been
deemed a piece of unchristian presumption.

THE
Legend of Saint Nicholas

Everybody has heard of St. Nicholas, that honest Dutch saint, whom I look upon as having been one of the most liberal, good-natured little fat fellows in the world. But, strange as it may seem, though everybody has heard, nobody seems to know anything about him. The place of his birth, the history of his life, and the manner in which he came to be the dispenser of Newyear cakes, and the patron of good boys, are matters that have hitherto not been investigated, as they ought to have been long and long ago. I am about to supply this deficiency, and pay a debt of honour which is due to this illustrious and obscure tutelary genius of the jolly Newyear.

It hath often been justly remarked that the birth, parentage, and education of the most illustrious personages of antiquity, are usually enveloped in the depths of obscurity. And this obscurity, so far from being injurious to their dignity and fame, has proved highly beneficial; for as no one could tell who were their fathers and mothers on earth, they could the more easily claim kindred with the skies, and trace their descent from the immortals. Such was the case with Saturn, Hercules, Bacchus, and others among the heathens; and of St. George, St. Dennis, St. Andrew, St. Patrick, and the rest of the tutelaries, of whom—I speak it with great respect and reverence—it may justly be said that nobody would ever have heard of their progenitors but for the renown of their descendants. It is, therefore, no reflection on the respectable St. Nicholas, that his history has hitherto remained a secret, and his origin unknown.

In prosecuting this biography, and thus striving to repay my obligations for divers, and I must say unmerited favours received from this good saint, after whom I was christened, I shall refrain from all invention or hyperbole, seeking the truth industriously, and telling it simply and without reserve or embellishment. I scorn to impose on my readers with cock and bull stories of his killing dragons, slaughtering giants, or defeating whole armies of pagans with his single arm. St. Nicholas was a peaceful, quiet, orderly saint, who, so far as I have been able to learn, never shed a drop of blood in his whole life, except, peradventure, it may be possible he sometimes cut his finger, of which I profess to know nothing, and therefore, contrary to the custom of biographers, shall say nothing.

St. Nicholas was born—and that is all I can tell of the matter—on the first of January; but in what year or at what place, are facts which I have not been able to ascertain, although I have investigated them with the most scrupulous accuracy. His obscurity would enable me to give him a king and queen for his parents, whereby he might be able to hold up his head with the best of them all; but, as I before observed, I scorn to impose such doubtful, to say no worse, legends upon my readers.

Nothing is known of his early youth, except that it hath come down to us that his mother dreamed, the night before his birth, that the sun was changed into a vast Newyear cake and the stars into *oily cooks* —which she concluded was the reason they burned so bright. It hath been shrewdly intimated by certain would-be antiquaries, who doubtless wanted to appear wiser than they really were, that because our worthy saint was called Nicholas, that must of course have been the name of his father. But I set such conjectures at naught, seeing that if all the sons were called after their fathers, the distinction of senior and junior would no longer be sufficient, and they would be obliged to number them as they do in the famous island of Nantucket, where I hear there are thirty-six Isaac Coffins and sixteen Pelegs.

Now, of the first years of the life of good St. Nicholas, in like manner, we have been able to learn nothing until he was apprenticed to a baker in the famous city of Amsterdam, after which this metropolis was once called, but which my readers doubtless know was christened over again when the English usurped possession, in the teeth of the great right of discovery derived from the illustrious navigator, Henricus Hudson, who was no more an Englishman than I am.

Whether the youth Nicholas was thus apprenticed to a baker on account of his mother's dream, or from his great devotion to Newyear cakes, which may be inferred from the bias of his after life, it is impossible to tell at this distant period. It is certain, however, that he was so apprenticed, and that is sufficient to satisfy all reasonable readers. As for those pestilent, curious, prying people, who want to know the why and wherefore of everything, we refer them to the lives of certain famous persons, which are so intermingled and confounded with the lives of their contemporaries, and the events, great and small, which happened in all parts of the world during their sojourn on the earth, that it is utterly impossible to say whose life it is we are reading. Many people of little experience take the title page for a guide, not knowing, peradventure, they might almost as safely rely upon history for a knowledge of the events of past ages.

Little Nicholas, our hero, was a merry, sweet-tempered caitiff, which was, doubtless, somewhat owing to his living almost altogether upon sweet things. He was marvellously devoted to cakes, and ate up numberless gingerbread alphabets before he knew a single letter.

Passing over the intermediate years, of which, indeed, I know no more than the man in the moon, I come to the period when, being twenty-four, and the term of his apprenticeship almost out, he fell desperately in love with the daughter of his worthy master, who was a burgomaster of forty years standing. In those unprecocious times, the boys did not grow to be men and the girls women, so soon as they do now. It would have been considered highly indecent for the former to think of falling in love before they were out of their time, or the latter to set up for young women before they knew how to be anything else. But as soon as the worthy Nicholas arrived at the age of twenty-four, being, as I said, within a year of the expiration of his time, he thought to himself that Katrinchee, or Catharine, as the English call it, was a clever, notable little soul, and eminently calculated to make him a good wife. This was the main point in the times of which I am speaking, when people actually married without first running mad either for love or money.

Katrinchee was the toast of all the young bakers of Amsterdam, and honest Nicholas had as many rivals as there were loaves of bread in that renowned city. But he was as gallant a little Dutchman as ever smoked his way through the world pipe foremost, and did not despair of getting the better of his rivals, especially as he was a great favourite with the burgo-master, as, indeed, his conduct merited. Instead of going the vulgar way to work, and sighing and whin-ing out romance in her ear, he cunningly, being doubtless inspired by Cupid himself, proceeded to insinuate his passion, and make it known by degrees to the pretty little Katrinchee, who was as plump as a partridge and had eyes of the colour of a clear sky.

First did he bake a cake in the shape of a heart pierced half through by a toasting fork, the which he presented her smoking hot, which she received with

a blush and did eat, to the great encouragement of
the worthy Nicholas. A month after, for he did not
wish to alarm the delicacy of the pretty Katrinchee,
he did bake another cake in the shape of two hearts,
entwined prettily with a true lover's knot. This, too,
she received with a blush, and did eat with marvellous content. After the expiration of a like period, he
did contrive another cake in the shape of a letter,
on which he had ingeniously engraven the following
couplet:

Wer diesen glauben wöhlt hat die vernanft verschworen,
Dem denken abgesaght sein eigentham verlohren.

The meaning of which, if the reader doth not comprehend, I do hereby earnestly advise him to set
about the Dutch language forthwith, that he may
properly appreciate its hidden beauties.

Little Katrinchee read this poesy with a sigh, and
rewarded the good Nicholas with a look which, as he
afterward affirmed, would have heated an oven.

Thus did the sly youth gradually advance himself
in the good graces of the little damsel, until at length
he ventured a downright declaration, in the shape of
a cake made in the exact likeness of a little Dutch
Cupid. The acceptance of this was conclusive, and

was followed by permission to address the matter to the decision of the worthy burgomaster, whose name I regret hath not come down to the present time.

The good man consulted his pipe, and after six months' hard smoking, came to the conclusion that the thing was feasible. Nicholas was a well-behaved, industrious lad, and the burgomaster justly concluded that the possession of virtuous and industrious habits without houses and lands, was better than houses and lands without them. So he gave his consent like an honest and ever-to-be-respected magistrate.

The news of the intended marriage spoiled all the bread baked in Amsterdam that day. The young bakers were so put out that they forgot to put yeast in their bread, and it was all heavy. But the hearts of the good Nicholas and his bride were as light as a feather notwithstanding, and when they were married it was truly said there was not a handsomer couple in all Amsterdam.

They lived together happily many years, and nothing was wanting to their felicity but a family of little chubby boys and girls. But it was ordained that he never should be blessed with any offspring, seeing that he was predestined to be the patron and benefactor of the children of others, not of his own. In good

time, and in the fullness of years, the burgomaster
died, leaving his fortune and his business to Nicholas, who had ever been a kind husband to his daughter, and a dutiful son to himself. Rich and liberal, it
was one of the chief pleasures of the good Nicholas to
distribute his cakes, of which he baked the best in all
Amsterdam, to the children of the neighbourhood,
who came every morning, and sometimes in the evening; and Nicholas felt his heart warm within his
bosom when he saw how they ate and laughed, and
were as happy, ay, and happier, too, than so many
little kings. The children all loved him, and so did
their fathers and mothers, so that in process of time
he was made a burgomaster, like his father-in-law
before him.

Not only did he entertain the jolly little folk of
the city in the manner heretofore described, but his
home was open to all travellers and sojourners who
had no other home, as well as those who came recommended from afar off. In particular the good pilgrims
of the church, who went about preaching and propa-
gating the true faith, by the which I mean the doctrines of the illustrious reformers in all time past.

The good Nicholas had, in the latter part of his
life, embraced these doctrines with great peril to
himself, for sore were the persecutions they under-

went in those days who departed from the crying abominations of the ancient church; and had it not been for the good name he had established in the city of Amsterdam, among all classes, high and low, rich and poor, he might, peradventure, have suffered at the stake. But he escaped, as it were, by a miracle, and lived to see the truth triumph at last even throughout all the land.

But before this came to pass his faithful and affectionate helpmate had been taken from him by death, sorely to his grief; and he would have stood alone in the world had it not been for the little children, now grown up to be men and women, who remembered his former kindness, and did all they could to console him—for such is ever the reward of kindness to our fellow-creatures.

One night as he was sitting disconsolate at home, thinking of poor Katrinchee, and wishing that either she was with him or he with her, he heard a distant uproar in the street, which seemed approaching nearer and nearer. He was about to rise and go to the door to see what was the occasion, when suddenly it was pushed open with some violence, and a man rushed past him with very little ceremony. He seemed in a great hurry, for he panted for breath, and it was some time before he could say,

"I beseech thee to shut the door and hide me, for my life is in danger."

Nicholas, who never refused to do a good-natured act, did as he was desired, so far as shutting and barring the door. He then asked,

"What hath endangered thy life, and who art thou, friend, that thou art thus afraid?"

"Ask me not now, I beseech thee, Nicholas—"

"Thou knowest my name then?" said the other, interrupting him.

"I do—everybody knows thee, and thy kindness of heart. But ask me nothing now—only hide me for the present, and when the danger is past I will tell thee all."

"Thou art no murderer or fugitive from justice?"

"No, on my faith. I am sinned against, but I never injured but one man, and I was sorry for that. But hark, I hear them coming—wilt thou or wilt thou not protect me?"

"I will," said the good Nicholas, who saw in the dignified air and open countenance of the stranger something that inspired both confidence and awe. Accordingly he hastily led him into a remote apartment, where he secreted him in a closet, the door of which could not be distinguished, and in which he kept his money and valuables, for he said to himself,

I will trust this man, he does not look as if he would abuse my confidence.

"Take this key and lock thyself in, that thou mayst be able to get out in case they take me away."

Presently there was heard a great hallooing and banging at the outward door, with a cry of "Open! open!" and Nicholas went to the door and opened it. A flood of people rushed in helter-skelter, demanding the body of an arch heretic, who, they said, had been seen to take refuge in the house. But with all their rage and eagerness, they begged his excuse for this unceremonious proceeding, for Nicholas was beloved and respected by all, though he was a heretic himself.

"He's here—we saw him enter!" they cried.

"If he is here, find him," quoth Nicholas, quietly. "I will not say he is not here, neither would I betray him if he were."

The interlopers then proceeded to search all parts of the house, except the secret closet, which escaped their attention. When they had done this, one of them said:

"We have heard of thy having a secret place in thy house where thy money and papers are secured. Open it to us—we swear not to molest or take away aught that is thine."

The good Nicholas was confounded at this de-

mand, and stood for a moment not knowing what to
say or what to do. The stranger in the closet heard it
too; but he was a stout-hearted man, and trusted in
the Lord.

"Where is thy strong closet?" cried one of the
fiercest and most forward of the intruders. "We must
and will find it."

"Well, then, find it," quoth Nicholas, quietly.

They inspected the room narrowly, and knocked
against the walls in hopes the hollow sound would
betray the secret of the place. But they were disappointed, for the door was so thick that it returned no
hollow sound.

They now began to be impatient, and savage
withal, and the ferocious leader exclaimed,

"Let us take this fellow then. One heretic is as
good as another—as bad I mean."

"Seize him!" cried another.

"To the stake!" cried a third.

They forgot the ancient kindness of the good
man; for bigotry and over-heated zeal remember not
benefits, and pay no respect to the obligations of
gratitude. The good Nicholas was violently seized,
his hands tied behind him, and he was about to be
carried away a sacrifice to the demon of religious
discord, when the door of the closet flew open and

the stranger came forth with a step so firm, a look so lofty and inspired, that the rabble quailed and were silent before him.

"Unbind this man," said he, in a voice of authority, "and bind me in his stead."

Not a man stirred. They seemed spell bound, and stood looking at each other in silent embarrassment.

"Unbind this man, I say!"

Still they remained, as it were, petrified with awe and astonishment.

"Well, then, I shall do it myself," and he proceeded to release the good Nicholas from his bonds, while the interlopers remained silent and motionless.

"Mistaken men!" then said he, looking at them with pity mingled with indignation, "you believe yourselves fulfilling the duties of your faith when you chase those who differ from you about the world, as if they were wild beasts, and drag them to the stake, like malefactors who have committed the worst crimes against society. You think that the blood of human victims is the most acceptable offering to your Maker, and worse than the ignorant pagans, who made martyrs of the blessed saints, sacrifice them on the altar of a religion which is all charity, meekness, and forgiveness. But I see you are ashamed of yourselves. Go, and do so no more."

The spirit of intolerance quailed before the majesty of truth and genius. The poor deluded men, whose passions had been stimulated by mistaken notions of religious duty, bowed their heads and departed, rebuked and ashamed.

"Who art thou?" asked Nicholas, when they were gone.

"Thou shalt soon know," replied the stranger. "In the mean time listen to me. I must be gone before the fiend, which I have, perhaps, only laid for a few moments, again awakens in the bosoms of these deluded men, or some others like them get on the scent of their prey, and track their victim hither. Listen to me, Nicholas, kind and good Nicholas. Thou wouldst have endangered thy own life for the safety of a stranger—one who had no claim on thee save that of hospitality—nay, not even that, for I was not thy guest by invitation, but intrusion. Blessed be thee and thine, thy house, thy memory when thou art dead, and thy lot hereafter. Thou art worthy to know who I am."

He then disclosed to him a name with which the world hath since rung, from clime to clime, from country to country. A name incorporated inseparably with the interests of truth and the progress of learning.

"Tell it not in Gath—proclaim it not in the streets of Askalon," continued he, "for it is a name which carries with it the sentence of death in this yet benighted city. Interests of the deepest nature—interests vitally connected with the progress of truth—the temporal and eternal happiness of millions living, of millions yet unborn, brought me hither. The business I came upon is in part performed; but it is now known to some that I am or have been in the city, who will never rest till they run me down and tear me in pieces. Farewell, and look for thy reward, if not here, hereafter—for, sure as thou livest and breathest, a good action, done with a pure and honest motive, is twice blessed—once to the doer and once to him to whom it is done."

The good Nicholas would have knelt to the mighty genius that stood before him, but he prevented him.

"I am no graven image, nor art thou an idolater that thou shouldst kneel to me. Farewell! Let me have thy prayers, for the prayers of a good man are indeed blessings."

Saying this, the illustrious stranger departed in haste, and Nicholas never saw him more for a long time. But he said to himself,

"Blessed is my house, for it hath sheltered the bright light of the universe."

From that time forward, he devoted himself to the good cause of the Reformation with heart and soul. His house was ever the refuge of the persecuted; his purse the never-failing resource of the distressed; and many were the victims of bigotry and intolerance whom his influence and entreaties saved from the stake and the torture. He lived a blessing to all within the sphere of his influence, and was blessed in living to see the faith which he loved and cherished at length triumph over the efforts of power, the arts of intrigue, and the fire of bigotry.

Neither did he forget or neglect the customary offices of kindness and good will to the little children of the city, who continued still to come and share his goodly cakes, which he gave with the smile and the open hand of kind and unaffected benignity. It must have been delightful to see the aged patriarch sitting at his door, while the little boys and girls gathered together from all parts to share his smiles, to be patted on the head, and kissed, and laden with his bounties.

Every Newyear's day especially, being his birth-day, as it came round, was a festival, not only to all the children but to all that chose to come and see him. It seemed that he grew younger instead of older on each return of the season; for he received every one with smiles, and even his enemies were welcome to his good cheer. He had not the heart to hate anybody on the day which he had consecrated to innocent gayety, liberal hospitality, and universal benevolence. In process of time, his example spread among the whole city, and from thence through the country, until every village and town, nay, every house, adopted the good custom of setting apart the first day of the year to be gay and happy, to exchange visits, and to shake hands with friends and forgive enemies.

Thus the good Nicholas lived, blessing all and blessed by all, until he arrived at a happy old age. When he had reached fourscore years, he was sitting by himself late in the evening of the first of January, old style, which is the only true and genuine era after all—the new style being a pestilent popish innovation—he was sitting, I say, alone, the visitors having all departed, laden with gifts and good wishes. A knock was heard at the door, which always opened of itself, like the heart of its owner, not only on New-year's day, but every day in the year.

A stately figure entered and sat down by him, after shaking his hand right heartily. The good Nicholas was now old, and his eyesight had somewhat failed him, particularly at night.

"Thou art welcome," quoth the old man.

"I know it," replied the other, "every one is welcome to the house of the good Nicholas, not only this, but every other day. I have heard of thee in my travels."

"Thou knowest my name—may I not know thine?"

The stranger whispered a name in his ear, which made the heart of the good Nicholas leap in his bosom.

"Dost thou remember the adventure of the closet?" said the stranger.

"Yea—blessed be the day and the hour," said the old man.

And now they had a long conversation, which pertained to high matters not according with the nature of my story, and therefore I pass them by, more especially as I do not exactly know what they were.

"I almost fear to ask thee," at length said Nicholas; "but wilt thou partake of my cheer, on this the day of my birth? I shall not live to see another."

Old people are often prophetic on the duration of their lives.

"Assuredly," replied the other, "for it is neither beneath my character nor calling to share the good man's feast, and to be happy when I can."

So they sat down together and talked of old times, and how much better the new times were than the old, inasmuch as the truth had triumphed, and they could now enjoy their consciences in peace.

The illustrious visitor staid all night; and the next morning, as he was about to depart, the aged Nicholas said to him,

"Farewell—I shall never see thee again. Thou art going a long journey, thou sayst, but I am about venturing on one yet longer."

"Well, be it so," said the other. "But those who remain behind will bless thy name and thy memory. The little children will love thee, and so long as thy countrymen cherish their ancient customs, thou wilt not be forgotten."

They parted, and the prediction of the good Nicholas was fulfilled. He fell asleep in the arms of death, who called him so softly, and received him so gently in his embrace, that though his family knew he slept, they little thought it was forever.

When this news went abroad into the city, you might see the worthy burgomasters and citizens knocking the ashes out of their pipes, and putting

them quietly by in their buttonholes; and the good
housewives ever and anon lifting their clean white
aprons to their eyes, that they might see to thread
their needles or find the stitches, as they sat knitting
their stockings. The shops and schools were all shut
the day he was buried; and it was remarked that the
men neglected their usual amusements, and the little
children had no heart to play.

When the whole city had gathered together at
the side of his grave, there suddenly appeared among
them a remarkable and goodly-looking man, of most
reverent demeanour. Every one bowed their bodies,
in respectful devotion, for they knew the man, and
what they owed him. All was silent as the grave just
about to receive the body of Nicholas, when he I have
just spoken of lifted his head, and said as follows:

"The good man just about to enter the narrow
house never defrauded his neighbour, never shut his
door on the stranger, never did an unkind action, nor
ever refused a kind one either to friend or foe. His
heart was all goodness, his faith all purity, his morals
all blameless, yea, all praiseworthy. Such a man deserves the highest title that can be bestowed on man.
Join me then, my friends, old and young—men,
women, and children, in blessing his memory as *the
good St. Nicholas;* for I know no better title to such a

distinction than pure faith, inflexible integrity, and active benevolence." Thus spake the great reformer, John Calvin.

The whole assembled multitude, with one voice and one heart, cried out, "Long live the blessed memory of the good St. Nicholas!" as they piously consigned him to the bosom of his mother earth.

Thus did he come to be called St. Nicholas; and the people, not content with this, as it were by a mutual sympathy, and without coming to any understanding on the subject, have ever since set apart the birthday of the good man for the exercise of hospitality to men, and gifts to little children. From the Old World they carried the custom to the New, where their posterity still hold it in reverence, and where I hope it will long continue to flourish, in spite of the cold heartless forms, unmeaning ceremonies, and upstart pretensions of certain vulgar people, who don't know any better, and therefore ought to be pitied for their ignorance, rather than condemned for their presumption.

Claas Schlaschenschlinger

Thrice blessed St. Nicholas! may thy memory and thine honours endure for ever and a day! It is true that certain arch calumniators, such as Romish priests and the like, have claimed thee as a Catholic saint, affirming with unparalleled insolence that ever since the pestilent heresy of the illustrious John Calvin, there hath not been so much as a single saint in the Reformed Dutch Church. But beshrew these keepers of fasts and other abominations, the truth is not, never was, nor ever will be in their mouths, or their hearts! Doth not everybody know that the blessed St. Nicholas was of the Reformed Dutch Church, and that the cunning Romanists did incontinently filch him from us to keep their own calendar in countenance? The splutterkins! But I will restrain the outpourings of my wrath, and contenting myself with having proved that the good saint was of the true faith, proceed with my story, which is of undoubted authority, since I had it from a descendant of Claas Schlaschenschlinger himself, who lives in great honour and glory at the Waalboght on Long Island, and is moreover a justice of the peace and deacon of the church.

Nicholas, or, according to the true orthography, Claas Schlaschenschlinger, was of a respectable parentage, being born at Saardam in our good faderland, where his ancestors had been proprietors of the greatest windmill in all the country round, ever since the period when that bloody tyrant, Philip of Spain, was driven from the Low Countries by the invincible valour of the Dutch, under the Prince of Orange. It is said in a certain credible tradition, that one of the family had done a good turn to the worshipful St. Nicholas, in secreting him from the persecutions of the Romanists, who now, forsooth, claim him to themselves! and that ever afterwards the saint took special interest and cognizance in their affairs.

While at Saardam, Little Claas, who was the youngest of a goodly family of seventeen children, was observed to be a great favourite of St. Nicholas, whose namesake he was, who always brought him a cake or two extra at his Christmas visits, and otherwise distinguished him above his brothers and sisters;

whereat they were not a little jealous, and did sometimes slyly abstract some of the little rogue's benefactions, converting them to their own comfort and recreation.

In the process of time, Claas grew to be a stout lad, and withal a little wild, as he did sometimes neglect the great windmill, the which he had charge of in turn with the rest of his brothers, whereby it more than once came to serious damage. Upon these occasions, the worthy father, who had a reverend care of the morals of his children, was accustomed to give him the bastinado; but as Claas wore a competent outfit of breeches, he did not much mind it, not he; only it made him a little angry, for he was a boy of great spirit. About the time, I say, that Claas had arrived at the years of two or three and twenty, and was considered a stout boy for his age, there was great talk of settling a colony at the Manhadoes, which the famous Heinrick Hudson had discovered long years before. Many people of good name and substance were preparing to emigrate there, seeing it was described as a land flowing with milk and honey —that is to say, abounding in shad and herrings— and affording mighty bargains of beaver and other skins.

Now Claas began to cherish an earnest longing

to visit these parts, for he was tired of tending the windmill, and besides he had a natural love for marshes and creeks, and being a shrewd lad, concluded that there must be plenty of these where beavers and such like abounded. But his father and the Vrouw Schlaschenschlinger did eschew and anathematize this notion of Claas's, and placed him apprentice to an eminent shoemaker, to learn that useful art and mystery. Claas considered it derogatory to the son of the proprietor of the greatest windmill in all Saardam to carry the lapstone, and wanted to be a doctor, a lawyer, or some such thing. But his father told him in so many words that there were more lawyers than clients in the town already, and that a good cobbler saved more people from being sick, than all the doctors cured. So Claas became apprentice to the shoemaking business, and served out his time, after which he got to be his own master, and determined to put in practice his design of visiting the Manhadoes, of which he had never lost sight.

After much ado, Mynheer Schlaschenschlinger, and the good vrouw, consented unwillingly to let him follow the bent of his inclinations, and accordingly all things were got ready for his departure for the New World, in company with a party which was going out under that renowned Lord Michael Paauw, who was proceeding to settle his domain of Pavonia, which lieth directly opposite to New-Amsterdam. Mynheer Schlaschenschlinger fitted out his son nobly, as becoming the owner of the largest windmill in all Saardam, equipping him with awls, and knives, and wax, and thread, together with a bench and a goodly lapstone, considering in his own mind that the great scarcity of stones in Holland might, peradventure, extend to the Manhadoes. Now all being prepared, it was settled that Claas should depart on the next day but one, the next being St. Nicholas his day, and a great festival among the people of Holland.

According to custom, ever since the days of the blessed saint, they had a plentiful supper of waffles and chocolate—that pestilent beverage tea not having yet come into fashion—and sat up talking of Claas, his adventures, and what he would see and hear in the Manhadoes, till it was almost nine o'clock. Upon this, mynheer ordered them all to bed, being scandalized at such unseasonable hours. In the morning when Claas got up and went to put on his stocking, he felt something hard at the toe, and turning it inside out, there fell on the floor the bowl of a pipe of the genuine *meershaum,* which seemed to have been used beyond memory, since its polish was a

thousand times more soft and delightsome than ivory
or tortoise shell, and its lustre past all price. Would
that the blessed saint would bestow such a one on
me!

Claas was delighted; he kissed it as if he had been
an idolatrous Romanist—which, by the blessing of
St. Nicholas, he was not—and bestowing it in the
bottom of his strong oaken chest, resolved, like unto
a prudent Dutchman, never to use it, for fear of
accidents. In a few hours afterwards, he parted from
his parents, his family, and his home; his father gave
him a history of the bloody wars and persecutions of
Philip of Spain, a small purse of guilders, and abun-
dance of advice for the government of his future life;
but his mother gave him what was more precious
than all these—her tears, her blessing, and a little
Dutch Bible with silver clasps. Bibles were not so
plenty then as they are now, and were considered as
the greatest treasures of the household. His brothers
and sisters took an affectionate farewell of him, and
asked his pardon for stealing his Newyear cookies.
So Claas kissed his mother, promising, if it pleased
Heaven, to send her stores of herrings and beaver
skins, whereat she was marvellously comforted; and
he went on his way, as it were sorrowfully rejoicing.

I shall pass over the journey, and the voyage to

the Manhadoes, saving the relation of a curious matter that occurred after the ship had been about ninety
days at sea, and they were supposed to be well on
their way to the port of New-Amsterdam. It came
into the heads of the passengers to while away the
time as they were lying-to one day with sails all
furled, except one or two, which I name not, for a
special reason, contrary to the practice of most writers—namely, because I am ignorant thereof—having
the sails thus furled, I say, on account of certain
suspicious-looking clouds, the which the captain,
who kept a bright lookout day and night, had seen
hovering overhead with no good intentions, it came
into the noddles of divers of the passengers to pass
the time by opening their chests and comparing their
respective outfits, for they were an honest set of people, and not afraid of being robbed.

When Claas showed his lapstone, most of the
company, on being told the reasons for bringing it
such a long distance, held up their hands, and ad-
mired the foresight of his father, considering him an
exceeding prudent and wise man to think of such
matters. Some of them wanted to buy it on specula-
tion, but Claas was too well acquainted with its value
to set a price on it. While they were thus chaffering,
an old sailor, who had accompanied the renowned

Heinrick Hudson as cabin boy in his first voyage to the Manhadoes, happening to come by and hear them, swore a great Dutch oath, and called Claas a splutterkin for bringing stones all the way from Holland, saying that there were enough at the Manhadoes to furnish lapstones for the whole universe. Whereupon Claas thought to himself, "What a fine country it must be, where stones are so plenty."

In the process of time, as all things, and especially voyagings by sea, have an end, the vessel came in sight of the highlands of Neversink—vulgarly called by would-be learned writers, Navesink—and Claas and the rest, who had never seen such vast mountains before, did think that it was a wall, built up from the earth to the sky, and that there was no world beyond. Favoured by a fine south wind, whose balmy freshness had awakened the young spring into early life and beauty, they shot like an arrow from a bow through the Narrows, and sailing along the heights of Staaten Island, came in sight of the illustrious city of New-Amsterdam, which, though at that period containing but a few hundred people, I shall venture to predict, in some future time, may actually number its tens of thousands.

Truly it was a beautiful city, and a beautiful sight as might be seen of a spring morning. As they came

through Buttermilk Channel, they beheld with delighted astonishment the fort, the church, the gover-
nor's house, the great dock jutting out into the salt
river, the Stadt Huys, the rondeel, and a goodly
assemblage of houses with the gable ends to the
street, as before the villainous introduction of new
fashions, and at the extremity of the city, the gate
and wall, from whence Wall-street deriveth its name.
But what above all gloriously delighted Claas, was a
great windmill, towering in the air, and spreading its
vast wings on the rising ground along the Broadway,
between Liberty and Courtlandt streets, the which
reminded him of home and his parents. The prospect
rejoiced them all mightily, for they thought to themselves, "We have come to a little Holland far over
the sea."

So far as I know, it was somewhere about the year
of our Lord one thousand six hundred and sixty, or
thereabout, and in the month of May, that Claas
landed in the New World; but of the precise day of
the month I cannot be certain, seeing what confusion
of dates hath been caused by that idolatrous device of
Pope Gregory called the New Style, whereby events
that really happened in one year are falsely put down
to another, by which means history becomes naught.
The first thing he thought of, was to provide himself

a home, for be it known it was not then the fashion to live in taverns and boarding houses, and the man who thus demeaned himself was considered no better than he should be; nobody would trust or employ him, and he might consider it a special bounty of the good St. Nicholas if he escaped a ride on the wooden horse provided for the punishment of delinquents. So Claas looked out for a pleasant place whereon to pitch his tent. As he walked forth for this end, his bowels yearned exceedingly for a lot on the Broad-street, through which ran a delightful creek, crooked like unto a ram's horn, the sides of which were low, and, as it were, juicy with the salt water which did sometimes overflow them at spring tides, and the full of the moon. More especially the ferry house, with its never-to-be-forgotten weathercock, did incite him sorely to come and set himself down thereabout. But he was deterred by the high price of lots in that favoured region, seeing they asked him as much as five guilders for the one at the corner of the Broad and Wall streets, a most unheard-of price, and not to be thought of by a prudent man like Claas Schlaschenschlinger.

So he sought about elsewhere, though he often looked wistfully at the fair meads of the Broad-street, and nothing deterred him from ruining himself by gratifying his longings but the truly excellent expedient of counting his money, which I recommend to all honest people, before they make a bargain. But though he could not settle in Broad-street, he resolved in his mind to get as nigh as possible, and finding a lot with a little puddle of brackish water in it large enough for a goose pond, nigh unto the wall and gate of the city, and just at the head of what hath lately been called New-street—then the region of unsettled lands—he procured a grant thereof from the schout, scheepens, and burgomasters who then ruled the city, for five stivers, being the amount of fees for writing and recording the deed by the Geheim Schryver.

Having built himself a comfortable house, with a little stoop to it, he purchased a pair of geese, or, to be correct and particular, as becometh a conscientious historian, a goose and gander, that he might recreate himself with their gambols in the salt puddle, and quietly sat himself down to the making and mending of shoes. In this he prospered at first indifferently well, and thereafter mightily, when the people found that he made shoes, some of which were reported never to wear out; but this was, as it were, but a sort of figure of speech to express their excellent qualities.

Every Sunday, after church, in pleasant weather,

Claas, instead of putting off his Sunday suit, as was the wont of the times, used to go and take a walk in the Ladies' Valley, since called Maiden Lane, for everything has changed under those arch intruders the English, who, I believe, in their hearts, are half Papists. This valley was an exceeding cool, retired, and pleasant place, being bordered by a wood, in the which was plenty of pinkster blossoms in the season. Being a likely young fellow, and dressed in a goodly array of breeches and what not, he was much noticed, and many a little damsel cast a sheep's eye upon him as he sat smoking his pipe of a summer afternoon under the shade of the trees which grew plentifully in that quarter. I don't know how it was, but so it happened, that in process of time he made acquaintance with one of these, a buxom creature of rare and unmatchable lineaments and dimensions, insomuch that she was considered the beauty of New-Amsterdam, and had refused even the burgomaster Barendt Roeloffsen, who was taxed three guilders, being the richest man of the city. But Aintjie was not to be bought with gold; she loved Claas because he was a solid young fellow, who plucked for her the most beautiful pinkster blossoms, and was the most pleasant companion in the world for a ramble in the Ladies' Valley.

Report says, but I believe there was no great truth in the story, that they sometimes QUEESTED * together, but of that I profess myself doubtful. Certain it is, however, that in good time they were married, to the great content of both, and the great discontent of the burgomaster Barendt Roeloffsen.

In those days young people did not marry to set up a coach, live in fine houses filled with rich furniture for which they had no use, and become bankrupt in a few years. They began in a small way, and increased their comforts with their means. It was thus with Claas and his wife, who were always employed in some useful business, and never ran into extravagance, except it may be on holydays. In particular Claas always feasted lustily on St. Nicholas his day, because he was his patron saint, and he remembered his kindness in faderland.

Thus they went on prospering as folks always do that are industrious and prudent, every year laying up money, and every year increasing their family; for be it known, those who are of the true Dutch blood always apportion the number of children to the means of providing for them. They never are caught having children for other people to take care of. But

---

* This word is untranslatable.

be this as it may, about this time began the mischievous and oppressive practice of improving the city, draining the marshes, cutting down hills, and straightening streets, which hath since grown to great enormity in this city, insomuch that a man may be said to be actually impoverished by his property.

Barendt Roeloffsen, who was at the head of the reformers, having a great estate in vacant lands which he wanted to make productive at the expense of his neighbours—Barendt Roeloffsen, I say, bestirred himself lustily to bring about what he called, in outlandish English, the era of improvement, and forthwith looked around to see where he should begin. I have always believed, and so did the people at that time, that Barendt singled out Claas his goose pond for the first experiment, being thereunto impelled by an old grudge against Claas, on account of his having cut him out with the damsel he wished to marry, as before related.

But, however, Barendt Roeloffsen, who bore a great sway among the burgomasters on account of his riches, got a law passed, by hook or by crook, for draining Claas his pond, at his own expense, making him pay at the same time for the rise in the value of his property, of which they did not permit him to be the judge, but took upon themselves to say what it was. The ancestors of Claas had fought valiantly against Philip of Spain, in defence of their religion and liberty, and he had kept up his detestation of oppression by frequently reading the account of the cruelties committed in the Low Countries by the Spaniard, in the book which his father had given him on his departure from home. Besides, he had a great admiration, I might almost say affection, for his goose pond, as is becoming in every true Dutchman. In it he was accustomed to see, with singular delight, his geese, now increased to a goodly flock, sailing about majestically, flapping their wings, dipping their necks into the water, and making a noise exceedingly tuneful and melodious. Here, too, his little children were wont to paddle in the summer days, up to their knees in the water, to their great contentment as well as recreation, thereby strengthening themselves exceedingly. Such being the case, Claas resisted the behest of the burgomasters, declaring that he would appeal to the laws for redress if they persisted in trespassing on his premises. But what can a man get by the law at any time, much less when the defendant, as in this case, was judge as well as a party in the business? After losing a vast deal of time, which was as money to him, and spending a good portion of what he had saved for his children,

Claas was at length cast in his suit, and the downfall of his goose pond irrevocably decreed.

It was a long time before he recovered from this blow, and when he did, Fortune, as if determined to persevere in her ill offices, sent a blacksmith from Holland who brought with him the new and diabolical invention of hobnails, the which he so strenuously recommended to the foolish people, who are prone to run after novelties, that they, one and all, had their shoes stuck full of nails, whereby they did clatter about the streets like unto a horse newly shod. As might be expected, the business of shoemaking decreased mightily upon this, insomuch that the shoes might be said to last for ever; and I myself have seen a pair that have descended through three generations, the nails of which shone like unto silver sixpences. Some people supposed this was a plot of Barendt Roeloffsen, to complete the ruin of poor Claas; but whether it was or not, it is certain that such was the falling off in his trade, on account of the pestilent introduction of hobnails, that at the end of the year Claas found that he had gone down hill at a great rate. The next year it was still worse, and thus, in the course of a few more, from bad to worse, he at last found himself without the means of support for himself, his wife, and his little children. But what shows the goodness of Providence, it is worthy of record that from this time his family, miraculously as it were, ceased to increase.

Neither begging nor running in debt without the prospect of paying was in fashion in those days, nor were there any societies to invite people to idleness and improvidence by the certainty of being relieved from their consequences without the trouble of asking. Claas tried what labouring day and night would do, but there was no use in making shoes when there was nobody to buy them. His good wife tried the magic of saving; but where there is nothing left to save, economy is to little purpose. He tried to get into some other business, but the wrath of Barendt Roeloffsen was upon him, and the whole influence of the burgomasters stood in his way on account of the opposition he had made to the march of improvement. He then offered his house and lot for sale; but here again his old enemy Barendt put a spoke in his wheel, going about among the people and insinuating that as Claas had paid nothing for his lot, the title was good for nothing. So one by one he tried all ways to keep want from his door; but it came at last, and one Newyear's eve, in the year of our Lord—I don't know what, the family was hovering round a miserable fire, not only without the customary means of enjoying the festivity of the season, but destitute of the very necessaries of life.

The evening was cold and raw, and the heavy moanings of a keen northeast wind announced the approach of a snow storm. The little children cowered over the almost expiring embers, shivering with cold and hunger; the old cat lay half buried in the ashes to keep herself warm; and the poor father and mother now looked at the little flock of ragged— no, not ragged—the mother took care of that; and industry can always ward off rags and dirt. But though not ragged or dirty, they were miserably clad and worse fed; and as the parents looked first at them and then at each other, the tears gathered in their eyes until they ran over.

"We must sell the silver clasps of the Bible my mother gave me, wife," said Claas, at last.

"The Goodness forbid," said she; "we should never prosper after it."

"We can't prosper worse than we do now, Aint-jie."

"You had better sell the little book about the murders of the Spaniards, that you sometimes read to me."

"It has no silver clasps, and will bring nothing," replied Claas, despondingly, covering his face with his hand, and seeming to think for a few moments. All at once he withdrew his hand, and cried,

"The pipe! the meershaum pipe! it is worth a hundred guilders!" and he ran to the place where he had kept it so carefully that he never used it once in the whole time he had it in his possession.

He looked at it wistfully, and it brought to his mind the time he found it in his stocking. He thought of his parents, his brothers, his sisters, and old faderland, and wished he had never parted from them to visit the New World. His wife saw what was passing in his heart, and said,

"Never mind, dear Claas, with these hundred guilders we shall get on again by the blessing of the good St. Nicholas, whose namesake you are."

Claas shook his head, and looked at the meershaum, which he could not bear to part with, because, somehow or other, he could not help thinking it was the gift of St. Nicholas. The wind now freshened, and moaned more loudly than ever, and the snow began to come in through the crevices of the door and windows. The cold increased apace, and the last spark of fire was expiring in the chimney. There was darkness without and within, for the candle, the last they had, was just going out.

Claas, without knowing what he was doing,

rubbed the pipe against his sleeve, as it were mechanically.

He had scarcely commenced rubbing, when the door suddenly opened, and without more ado, a little man with a right ruddy good-humoured face, as round as an apple, and a cocked beaver, white with snow, walked in, without so much as saying, "By your leave," and sitting himself by the side of the yffrouw, began to blow at the fire and make as if he was warming his fingers, though there was no fire there, for that matter.

Now Claas was a good-natured fellow, and though he had nothing to give, except a welcome, which is always in the power of everybody, yet he wished to himself he had more fire to warm people's fingers. After a few moments, the little man rubbed his hands together, and looking around him with a good-humoured smile, said,

"Mynheer Schlaschenschlinger, methinks it might not be amiss to replenish this fire a little; 'tis a bitter cold night, and my fingers are almost frostbitten."

"Alack, mynheer," quoth Claas, "I would, with all my heart, but I have nothing wherewith to warm myself and my children, unless I set fire to my own house. I am sorry I cannot entertain thee better."

Upon this the little man broke the cane with which he walked into two pieces, which he threw in the chimney, and thereupon the fire began to blaze so cheerfully that they could see their shadows on the wall, and the old cat jumped out of the ashes, with her coat well singed, which made the little jolly fellow laugh heartily.

The sticks burnt and burnt, without going out, and they were soon all as warm and comfortable as could be. Then the little man said,

"Friend Claas, methinks it would not be much amiss if the good vrouw here would bestir herself to get something to eat. I have had no dinner today, and come hither on purpose to make merry with thee. Knowest thou not that this is Newyear's eve?"

"Alack!" replied Claas, "I know it full well; but we have not wherewithal to keep away hunger, much less to make merry with. Thou art welcome to all we have, and that is nothing."

"Come, come, Friend Claas, thou art a prudent man, I know, but I never thought thou wert stingy before. Bestir thyself, good Aintjie, and see what thou canst find in that cupboard. I warrant there is plenty of good fare in it."

The worthy yffrouw looked rather foolish at this proposal, for she knew she would find nothing there if she went; but the little man threatened her, in a good-humoured way, to break the long pipe he carried stuck in his cocked hat over her nightcap, if she didn't do as he bid her. So she went to the cupboard, resolved to bring him out the empty pewter dishes, to show they had nothing to give him. But when she opened the cupboard, she started back, and cried out aloud, so that Claas ran to see what was the matter; and what was his astonishment to find the cupboard full of all sorts of good things for a notable jollification.

"Aha!" cried the merry little man, "you're caught at last. I knew thou hadst plenty to entertain a stranger withal; but I suppose thou wantedst to keep it all to thyself. Come, come! bestir thyself, Aintjie, for I am as hungry as a schoolboy."

Aintjie did as she was bid, wondering all the time who this familiar little man could be; for the city was not so big but that she knew by sight everybody that lived in it, and she was sure she had never seen him before.

In a short time there was a glorious array of good things set out before them, and they proceeded to enjoy themselves right lustily in keeping of the merry Newyear's eve. The little man cracked his jokes; patted little Nicholas—Claas, his youngest son, who

was called after his father—on the head; chucked
Aintjie under the chin; said he was glad she did not
wed the splutterkin Barendt Roeloffsen; and set them
so good an example, that they all got as merry as
crickets.

By-and-by the little man inquired of Claas concerning his affairs, and he gave him an account of his
early prosperity, and how he had declined, in spite of
all he could do, into poverty and want; so that he
had nothing left but his wife, his children, his Dutch
Bible, his history of the Low Country wars, and his
meershaum pipe.

"Aha!" quoth the little man, "you've kept that,
hey! Let me see it."

Claas gave it to him, while the tears came into
his eyes, although he was so merry, to think that he
must part with it on the morrow. It was the pride of
his heart, and he set too great a value on it to make
any use of it whatever.

The little man took the pipe, and looking at it,
said, as if to himself,

"Yes; here it is! the very identical meershaum out
of which the great Calvin used to smoke. Thou hast
done well, Friend Claas, to preserve it; and thou
must keep it as the apple of thine eye all thy life, and
give it as an inheritance to thy children."

"Alack!" cried Aintjie, "he must sell it to-mor-row, or we shall want wherewithal for a dinner."

"Yea," said Claas, "of a truth it must go to-morrow!"

"Be quiet, splutterkin!" cried the little man, merrily; "give me some more of that spiced beverage, for I am as thirsty as a dry sponge. Come, let us drink to the Newyear, for it will be here in a few minutes."

So they drank a cup to the jolly Newyear, and at that moment the little boys and negroes, who didn't mind the snow any more than a miller does flour, began to fire their cannon at a great rate; whereupon the little man jumped up, and cried out,

"My time is come! I must be off, for I have a great many visits to pay before sunrise."

Then he kissed the yffrouw with a hearty smack, just as doth the illustrious Rip Van Dam, on the like occasions; patted little Nicholas on the head, and gave him his blessing; after which he did inconti-nently leap up the chimney and disappear. Then they knew it was the good St. Nicholas, and rejoiced mightily in the visit he had paid them, looking upon it as an earnest that their troubles were over.

The next morning the prudent housewife, ac-cording to custom, got up before the dawn of day to put her house in order, and when she came to sweep the floor, was surprised to hear something jingle just like money. Then, opening the embers, the sticks which the good saint had thrown upon the fire again blazed out, and she descried a large purse, which on examination was found filled with golden ducats. Whereupon she called out to Claas, and they examined the purse, and found fastened to it a paper bearing this legend:

THE GIFT OF ST. NICHOLAS

While they stood in joyful wonder, they heard a great knocking and confusion of tongues outside the door, and the people calling aloud upon Claas Schlaschenschlinger to come forth; whereupon he went forth, and, to his great astonishment, found that his little wooden house had disappeared in the night, and in its place was standing a gorgeous and magnificent mansion of Dutch bricks, two stories high, with three windows in front, all of a different size, and a door cut right out of the corner, just as it is seen at this blessed day.

The neighbours wondered much, and it was whispered among them that the fiend had helped Claas to this great domicil, which was one of the biggest in the city, and almost equal to that of Barendt Roeloffsen. But when Claas told them of the visit of St. Nicholas, and showed them the purse of golden ducats, with the legend upon it, they thought better of it, and contented themselves with envying him heartily his good fortune.

I shall not relate how Claas prospered ever afterwards, in spite of his enemies the burgomasters, who at last were obliged to admit him as one of their number; or how little Aintjie held up her head among the highest; or how Claas ever after eschewed the lapstone, and, like a worshipful magistrate, took to bettering the condition of mankind, till at length he died, and was gathered to his forefathers, full of years and honours.

All I shall say is that the great house in Newstreet continued in the family for several generations, until a degenerate descendant of Claas, being thereunto incited by the d——l, did sell it to another degenerate splutterkin, who essayed to pull it down. But mark what followed. No sooner had the workmen laid hands on it, than the brickbats began to fly about at such a rate that they all came away faster than they went; some with broken heads, and others with broken bones, and not one could ever be persuaded to meddle with it afterwards.

And let this be a warning to any one who shall attempt to lay their sacrilegious hands on the LAST OF THE DUTCH HOUSES, the gift of St. Nicholas, for whoever does so may calculate, to a certainty, on getting well peppered with brickbats, I can tell them.

THE
Revenge of Saint Nicholas

Everybody knows that in the famous city of New-York, whose proper name is New-Amsterdam, the excellent St. Nicholas—who is worth a dozen St. Georges and dragons to boot, and who, if every tub stood on its right bottom, would be at the head of the Seven Champions of Christendom—I say, everybody knows the excellent St. Nicholas, in holyday times, goes about among the people in the middle of the night, distributing all sorts of toothsome and becoming gifts to the good boys and girls in this his favourite city. Some say that he comes down the chimneys in a little Jersey wagon; others, that he wears a pair of Holland skates, with which he travels like the wind; and others, who pretend to have seen him, maintain that he has lately adopted a locomotive, and was once actually detected on the *Albany* railroad.

But this last assertion is looked upon to be entirely fabulous, because St. Nicholas has too much discretion to trust himself in such a newfangled jarvie; and so I leave this matter to be settled by whosoever will take the trouble. My own opinion is that his favourite mode of travelling is on a canal, the motion and speed of which aptly comport with the philosophic dignity of his character. But this is not material, and I will no longer detain my readers with extraneous and irrelevant matters, as is too much the fashion with our statesmen, orators, biographers, and story tellers.

It was in the year one thousand seven hundred and sixty, or sixty-one, for the most orthodox chronicles differ in this respect; but it was a very remarkable year, and it was called *annus mirabilis* on that account. It was said that several people were detected in speaking the truth, about that time; that nine staid, sober, and discreet widows, who had sworn on an anti-masonic almanac never to enter a second time into the holy state, were snapped up by young husbands before they knew what they were about; that six venerable bachelors wedded as many buxom young belles, and, it is reported, were afterwards sorry for what they had done; that many people actually went to church from motives of piety; and that a great scholar, who had written a book in support of certain opinions, was not only convinced of his error, but acknowledged it publicly afterwards. No wonder the year one thousand seven hundred and sixty, if that was the year, was called *annus mirabilis!*

What contributed to render this year still more remarkable, was the building of six new three-story brick houses in the city, and three persons setting up equipages, who, I cannot find, ever failed in business afterwards, or compounded with their creditors at a pistareen in the pound. It is, moreover, recorded in the annals of the horticultural society of that day, which were written on a cabbage leaf, as is said, that a member produced a forked radish of such vast dimensions that, being dressed up in fashionable male attire at the exhibition, it was actually mistaken for a travelled beau by several inexperienced young ladies, who pined away for love of its beautiful complexion, and were changed into daffadowndillies. Some maintained it was a mandrake, but it was finally detected by an inquest of experienced matrons. No wonder the year seventeen hundred and sixty was called *annus mirabilis!*

But the most extraordinary thing of all, was the confident assertion that there was but one *gray mare* within the bills of mortality; and, incredible as it may appear, she was the wife of a responsible citizen, who, it was affirmed, had grown rich by weaving velvet purses out of sows' ears. But this we look upon as being somewhat of the character of the predictions of almanac makers. Certain it is, however, that Amos Shuttle possessed the treasure of a wife who was shrewdly suspected of having established within doors a system of government not laid down in Aristotle or the Abbe Sièyes, who made a constitution for every day in the year, and two for the first of April.

Amos Shuttle, though a mighty pompous little man out of doors, was the meekest of human creatures within. He belonged to that class of people who pass for great among the little, and little among the great; and he would certainly have been master in his own house had it not been for a woman! We have read somewhere that no wise woman ever thinks her husband a demigod. If so, it is a blessing that there are so few wise women in the world.

Amos had grown rich, Heaven knows how—he did not know himself; but, what was somewhat extraordinary, he considered his wealth a signal proof of his talents and sagacity, and valued himself according to the infallible standard of pounds, shillings, and pence. But though he lorded it without, he was, as we have just said, the most gentle of men within doors. The moment he stepped inside of his own house, his spirit cowered down, like that of a pious man entering a church; he felt as if he was in the presence of a superior being—to wit, Mrs. Abigail Shuttle. He was, indeed, the meekest of beings at home, except Moses; and Sir Andrew Aguecheek's song, which Sir Toby Belch declared "would draw nine souls out of one weaver," would have failed in drawing half a one out of Amos. The truth is, his wife, who ought to have known, affirmed he had no more soul than a monkey; but he was the only man in the city thus circumstanced at the time we speak of. No wonder, therefore, the year one thousand seven hundred and sixty was called *annus mirabilis!*

Such as he was, Mr. Amos Shuttle waxed richer and richer everyday, insomuch that those who envied his prosperity were wont to say, "that he had certainly been born with a dozen silver spoons in his mouth, or such a great blockhead would never have got together such a heap of money." When he had become worth ten thousand pounds, he launched his shuttle magnanimously out of the window, ordered his weaver's beam to be split up for oven wood, and Mrs. Amos turned his weaver's shop into a *boudoir*. Fortune followed him faster than he ran away from her. In a few years the ten thousand doubled, and in a few more trebled, quadrupled—in short, Amos could hardly count his money.

"What shall we do now, my dear?" asked Mrs. Shuttle, who never sought his opinion, that I can learn, except for the pleasure of contradicting him.

"Let us go and live in the country, and enjoy ourselves," quoth Amos.

"Go into the country! Go to—" I could never satisfy myself what Mrs. Shuttle meant; but she stopped short, and concluded the sentence with a withering look of scorn, that would have cowed the spirits of nineteen weavers.

Amos named all sorts of places, enumerated all sorts of modes of life he could think of, and every pleasure that might enter into the imagination of a man without a soul. His wife despised them all; she would not hear of them.

"Well, my dear, suppose you suggest something; do now, Abby," at length said Amos, in a coaxing whisper; "will you, my onydoney?"

"Ony fiddlestick! I wonder you repeat such vulgarisms. But if I must say what I should like, I should like to travel."

"Well, let us go and make a tour as far as Jamaica, or Hackensack, or Spiking-devil. There is excellent fishing for striped bass there."

"Spiking-devil!" screamed Mrs. Shuttle; "an't you ashamed to swear so, you wicked mortal! I won't go to Jamaica, nor Hackensack among the Dutch Hottentots, nor to Spiking-devil to catch striped bass. I'll go to Europe!"

If Amos had possessed a soul it would have jumped out of its skin at the idea of going beyond seas. He had once been on the sea-bass banks, and got a seasoning there; the very thought of which made him sick. But, as he had no soul, there was no great harm done.

When Mrs. Shuttle said a thing, it was settled. They went to Europe, taking their only son with them; the lady ransacked all the milliners' shops in Paris, and the gentleman visited all the restaurateurs. He became such a desperate connoisseur and gourmand, that he could almost tell an *omelette au jambon* from a gammon of bacon. After consummating the polish, they came home, the lady with the newest old fashions, and the weaver with a confirmed preference of *potage à la Turque* over pepper-pot. It is said the city trembled, as with an earthquake, when they landed; but the notion was probably superstitious.

They arrived near the close of the year, the memorable year, the *annus mirabilis,* one thousand seven hundred and sixty. Everybody that had ever known

the Shuttles flocked to see them, or rather to see what
they had brought with them; and such was the magic
of a voyage to Europe, that Mr. and Mrs. Amos
Shuttle, who had been nobodies when they departed,
became somebodies when they returned, and
mounted at once to the summit of *ton.*

"You have come in good time to enjoy the festivi-
ties of the holydays," said Mrs. Hubblebubble, an
old friend of Amos the weaver and his wife.

"We shall have a merry Christmas and a happy
Newyear," exclaimed Mrs. Doubletrouble, another
old acquaintance of old times.

"The holydays," drawled Mrs. Shuttle; "the holydays? Christmas and Newyear? Pray what are
they?"

It is astonishing to see how people lose their
memories abroad sometimes. They often forget their
old friends, old customs, and occasionally themselves.

"Why, la! now, who'd have thought it?" cried
Mrs. Doubletrouble; "why, sure you haven't forgot
the oily cooks and the mince pies, the merry meet-
ings of friends, the sleigh-rides, the Kissing Bridge,
and the family parties?"

"Family parties!" shrieked Mrs. Shuttle, and held
her salts to her nose; "family parties! I never heard of

anything so Gothic in Paris or Rome; and oily cooks —oh shocking! and mince pies—detestable! and throwing open one's doors to all one's old friends, whom one wishes to forget as soon as possible. Oh! the idea is insupportable!" and again she held the salts to her nose.

Mrs. Hubblebubble and Mrs. Doubletrouble found they had exposed themselves sadly, and were quite ashamed. A real, genteel, well-bred, enlightened lady of fashion ought to have no rule of conduct, no conscience, but Paris—whatever is fashionable there is genteel—whatever is not fashionable is vulgar. There is no other standard of right, and no other eternal fitness of things. At least so thought Mrs. Hubblebubble and Mrs. Doubletrouble.

"But is it possible that all these things are out of fashion abroad?" asked the latter, beseechingly.

"They never were in," said Mrs. Amos Shuttle. "For my part, I mean to close my doors and windows on Newyear's day—I'm determined."

"And so am I," said Mrs. Hubblebubble.

"And so am I," said Mrs. Doubletrouble.

And it was settled that they should make a combination among themselves and their friends, to put down the ancient and good customs of the city, and abolish the sports and enjoyments of the jolly Newyear. The conspirators then separated, each to pursue her diabolical designs against oily cooks, mince pies, sleigh ridings, sociable visitings, and family parties.

Now the excellent St. Nicholas, who knows well what is going on in every house in the city, though, like a good and honourable saint, he never betrays any family secrets, overheard these wicked women plotting against his favourite anniversary, and he said to himself,

"Vuur en Vlammen! but I'll be even with you, *mein vrouw."* So he determined he would play these conceited and misled women a trick or two before he had done with them.

It was now the first day of the new year, and Mrs. Amos Shuttle, and Mrs. Doubletrouble, and Mrs. Hubblebubble, and their wicked abetters, had shut up their doors and windows, so that when their old friends called they could not get into their houses. Moreover, they had prepared neither mince pies, nor oily cooks, nor crullers, nor any of the good things consecrated to St. Nicholas by his pious and well-intentioned votaries, and they were mightily pleased at having been as dull and stupid as owls, while all the rest of the city were as merry as crickets, chirping and frisking in the warm chimney corner. Little did they think what horrible judgments were impending

over them, prepared by the wrath of the excellent St.
Nicholas, who was resolved to make an example of
them for attempting to introduce their newfangled
corruptions in place of the ancient customs of his
favourite city. These wicked women never had another comfortable sleep in their lives!

The night was still, clear, and frosty—the earth
was everywhere one carpet of snow, and looked just
like the ghost of a dead world, wrapped in a white
winding sheet; the moon was full, round, and of a
silvery brightness, and by her discreet silence afforded an example to the rising generation of young
damsels, while the myriads of stars that multiplied
as you gazed at them seemed as though they were
frozen into icicles, they looked so cold, and sparkled
with such a glorious lustre. The streets and roads
leading from the city were all alive with sleighs filled
with jovial souls, whose echoing laughter and cheerful songs mingled with a thousand merry bells that
jingled in harmonious dissonance, giving spirit to
the horses and animation to the scene. In the license
of the season, hallowed by long custom, each of the
sleighs saluted the others in passing with a "Happy
Newyear," a merry jest, or mischievous gibe, ex-
changed from one gay party to another. All was life,
motion, and merriment; and as old frostbitten Win-

ter, aroused from his trance by the rout and revelry around, raised his weatherbeaten head to see what was passing, he felt his icy blood warming and coursing through his veins, and wished he could only overtake the laughing buxom Spring, that he might dance a jig with her, and be as frisky as the best of them. But as the old rogue could not bring this desirable matter about, he contented himself with calling for a jolly bumper of cocktail, and drinking a swinging draught to the health of the blessed St. Nicholas, and those who honour the memory of the president of good fellows.

All this time the wicked women and their abetters lay under the malediction of the good saint, who caused them to be bewitched by an old lady from Salem. Mrs. Amos Shuttle could not sleep, because something had whispered in her apprehensive ear that her son, her only son, whom she had engaged to the daughter of Count Grenouille, in Paris, then about three years old, was actually at that moment crossing Kissing Bridge in company with little Susan Varian, and some others besides. Now Susan was the fairest little lady of all the land; she had a face and an eye just like the Widow Wadman, in Leslie's charming picture; a face and an eye which no reasonable man under Heaven could resist, except my Uncle

Toby—beshrew him and his fortifications, I say! She was, moreover, a good little girl, and an accomplished little girl—but, alas! she had not mounted to the step in Jacob's ladder of fashion which qualifies a person for the heaven of high *ton,* and Mrs. Shuttle had not been to Europe for nothing. She would rather have seen her son wedded to dissipation and profligacy than to Susan Varian; and the thought of his being out sleigh-riding with her was worse than the toothache. It kept her awake all the livelong night; and the only consolation she had was scolding poor Amos, because the sleigh bells made such a noise.

As for Mrs. Hubblebubble and Mrs. Doubletrouble, they neither of them got a wink of sleep during a whole week, for thinking of the beautiful French chairs and damask curtains Mrs. Shuttle had brought from Europe. They forthwith besieged their good men, leaving them no rest until they sent out orders to Paris for just such rich chairs and curtains as those of the thrice happy Mrs. Shuttle, from whom they kept the affair a profound secret, each meaning to treat her to an agreeable surprise. In the mean while they could not rest for fear the vessel which was to bring these treasures might be lost on her passage. Such was the dreadful judgment inflicted on them by the good St. Nicholas.

The perplexities of Mrs. Shuttle increased daily. In the first place, do all she could, she could not make Amos a fine gentleman. This was a metamorphosis which Ovid would never have dreamed of. He would be telling the price of everything in his house, his furniture, his wines, and his dinners, insomuch that those who envied his prosperity, or, perhaps, only despised his pretensions, were wont to say, after eating his venison and drinking his old Madeira, "that he ought to have been a tavern keeper, he knew so well how to make out a bill." Mrs. Shuttle once overheard a speech of this kind, and the good St. Nicholas himself, who had brought it about, almost felt sorry for the mortification she endured on the occasion.

Scarcely had she got over this, when she was invited to a ball by Mrs. Hubblebubble, and the first thing she saw on entering the drawing room was a suit of damask curtains and chairs, as much like her own as two peas, only the curtains had far handsomer fringe. Mrs. Shuttle came very near fainting away, but escaped for that time, determining to mortify this impudent creature by taking not the least notice of her finery. But St. Nicholas ordered it otherwise, so that she was at last obliged to acknowledge they were very elegant indeed. Nay, this was not the worst, for she overhead one lady whisper to another that Mrs. Hubblebubble's curtains were much richer than Mrs. Shuttle's.

"Oh, I dare say," replied the other—"I dare say Mrs. Shuttle bought them second hand, for her husband is as mean as pursley."

This was too much. The unfortunate woman was taken suddenly ill—called her carriage, and went home, where it is supposed she would have died that evening had she not wrought upon Amos to promise her an entire new suit of French furniture for her drawing room and parlour to boot, besides a new carriage. But for all this she could not close her eyes that night for thinking of the "second-hand curtains."

Nor was the wicked Mrs. Doubletrouble a whit better off, when her friend Mrs. Hubblebubble treated her to the agreeable surprise of the French window curtains and chairs. "It is too bad—too bad, I declare," said she to herself; "but I'll pay her off soon." Accordingly, she issued invitations for a grand ball and supper, at which both Mrs. Shuttle and Mrs. Hubblebubble were struck dumb at beholding a suit of curtains and a set of chairs exactly of the same pattern with theirs. The shock was terrible, and it is impossible to say what might have been the consequences, had not the two ladies all at once thought of uniting in abusing Mrs. Doubletrouble for her extravagance.

"I pity poor Mr. Doubletrouble," said Mrs. Shuttle, shrugging her shoulders significantly, and glancing at the room.

"And so do I," said Mrs. Hubblebubble, doing the same.

Mrs. Doubletrouble had her eye upon them, and enjoyed their mortification until her pride was brought to the ground by a dead shot from Mrs. Shuttle, who was heard to exclaim, in reply to a lady who observed the chairs and curtains were very handsome,

"Why, yes; but they have been out of fashion in Paris a long time; and, besides, really they are getting so common, that I intend to have mine removed to the nursery."

Heavens! what a blow! Poor Mrs. Doubletrouble hardly survived it. Such a night of misery as the wicked woman endured almost made the good St. Nicholas regret the judgment he had passed upon these mischievous and conceited females. But he thought to himself he would persevere until he had made them a sad example to all innovators upon the ancient customs of our forefathers.

Thus were these wicked and miserable women spurred on by witchcraft from one piece of extravagance to another, and a deadly rivalship grew up between them, which destroyed their own happiness and that of their husbands. Mrs. Shuttle's new carriage and drawing-room furniture in due time were followed by similar extravagances on the part of the two other wicked women, who had conspired against the hallowed institutions of St. Nicholas; and soon their rivalship came to such a height that neither of them had a moment's rest or comfort from that time forward. But they still shut their doors on the jolly anniversary of St. Nicholas, though the old respectable burghers and their wives, who had held up their heads time out of mind, continued the good custom, and laughed at the presumption of these upstart interlopers, who were followed only by a few people of silly pretensions, who had no more soul than Amos Shuttle himself. The three wicked women grew to be almost perfect skeletons, on account of the vehemence with which they strove to outdo each other, and the terrible exertions necessary to keep up the appearance of being the best friends in the world. In short, they became the laughingstock of the town; and sensible, well-bred folks cut their acquaintance, except when they sometimes accepted an invitation to a party, just to make merry with their folly and conceitedness.

The excellent St. Nicholas, finding they still persisted in their opposition to his rites and ceremonies, determined to inflict on them the last and worst punishment that can befall the sex. He decreed that they should be deprived of all the delights springing from the domestic affections, and all taste for the innocent and virtuous enjoyments of a happy fireside. Accordingly, they lost all relish for home; were continually gadding about from one place to another in search of pleasure, and worried themselves to death to find happiness where it is never to be found. Their whole lives became one long series of disappointed hopes, galled pride, and gnawing envy. They lost their health, they lost their time, and their days became days of harassing impatience, their nights nights of sleepless, feverish excitement, ending in weariness and disappointment. The good saint sometimes felt sorry for them, but their continued obstinacy determined him to persevere in his plan to punish the upstart pride of these rebellious females.

Young Shuttle, who had a soul, which I suppose he inherited from his mother, all this while continued his attentions to little Susan Varian, which added to the miseries inflicted on his wicked mother. Mrs.

Shuttle insisted that Amos should threaten to disinherit his son, unless he gave up this attachment.

"Lord bless your soul, Abby," said Amos, "what's the use of my threatening, the boy knows as well as I do that I've no will of my own. Why, bless my soul, Abby—"

"Bless your soul!" interrupted Mrs. Shuttle; "I wonder who'd take the trouble to bless it but yourself? However, if you don't I will."

Accordingly, she threatened the young man with being disinherited unless he turned his back on little Susan Varian, which no man ever did without getting a heartache.

"If my father goes on as he has done lately," sighed the youth, "he won't have anything left to disinherit me of but his affection, I fear. But if he had millions I would not abandon Susan."

"Are you not ashamed of such a lowlived attachment? You, that have been to Europe! But, once for all, remember this, renounce this lowborn upstart, or quit your father's home for ever."

"Upstart!" thought young Shuttle; "one of the oldest families in the city." He made his mother a respectful bow, bade Heaven bless her, and left the house. He was however, met by his father at the door, who said to him,

"Johnny, I give my consent; but mind, don't tell your mother a word of the matter. I'll let her know I've a soul as well as other people"; and he tossed his head like a war horse.

The night after this Johnny was married to little Susan, and the blessing of affection and beauty lighted upon his pillow. Her old father, who was in a respectable business, took his son-in-law into partnership, and they prospered so well that in a few years Johnny was independent of all the world, with the prettiest wife and children in the land. But Mrs. Shuttle was inexorable, while the knowledge of his prosperity and happiness only worked her up to a higher pitch of anger, and added to the pangs of jealousy perpetually inflicted on her by the rivalry of Mrs. Hubblebubble and Mrs. Doubletrouble, who suffered under the like infliction from the wrathful St. Nicholas, who was resolved to make them an example to all posterity.

No fortune, be it ever so great, can stand the eternal sapping of wasteful extravagance, engendered and stimulated by the baleful passion of envy. In less than ten years from the hatching of the diabolical conspiracy of these three wicked women against the supremacy of the excellent St. Nicholas, their spend-

thrift rivalship had ruined the fortunes of their husbands, and entailed upon themselves misery and
remorse. Rich Amos Shuttle became at last as poor as
a church mouse, and would have been obliged to take
to the loom again in his old age had not Johnny, now
rich, and a worshipful magistrate of the city, afforded
him and his better half a generous shelter under his
own happy roof. Mrs. Hubblebubble and Mrs. Doubletrouble had scarcely time to condole with Mrs.
Shuttle, and congratulate each other, when their husbands went the way of all flesh, that is to say, failed
for a few tens of thousands, and called their creditors
together to hear the good news. The two wicked
women lived long enough after this to repent of their
offence against St. Nicholas; but they never imported
any more French curtains, and at last perished miserably in an attempt to set the fashions in Pennypot
alley.

Mrs. Abigail Shuttle might have lived happily
the rest of her life with her children and grandchildren, who all treated her with reverent courtesy and
affection, now that the wrath of the mighty St. Nicholas was appeased by her exemplary punishment. But
she could not get over her bad habits and feelings, or
forgive her lovely little daughter-in-law for treating

her so kindly when she so little deserved it. She gradually pined away; and though she revived at hearing of the catastrophe of Mrs. Hubblebubble and Mrs. Doubletrouble, it was only for a moment. The remainder of the life of this wicked woman was a series of disappointments and heartburnings, and when she died, Amos tried to shed a few tears, but he found it impossible, I suppose, because, as his wife always said, "he had no soul."

Such was the terrible revenge of St. Nicholas, which ought to be a warning to all who attempt to set themselves up against the venerable customs of their ancestors, and backslide from the hallowed institutions of the blessed saint, to whose good office, without doubt, it is owing that this his favourite city has transcended all others of the universe in beautiful damsels, valorous young men, mince pies, and New-year cookies. The catastrophe of these three wicked women had a wonderful influence in the city, insomuch that from this time forward, no *gray mares* were ever known, no French furniture was ever used, and no woman was hardy enough to set herself up in opposition to the good customs of St. Nicholas. And so, wishing many happy Newyears to all my dear countrywomen and countrymen, saving those who shut their doors to old friends, high or low, rich or poor, on that blessed anniversary, which makes more glad hearts than all others put together—I say, wishing a thousand happy Newyears to all, with this single exception, I lay down my pen, with a caution to all wicked women to beware of the revenge of St. Nicholas.

THE

Origin of the Baker's Dozen

Little Brom Boomptie, or Boss Boomptie, as he was commonly called by his apprentices and neighbours, was the first man that ever baked Newyear cakes in the good city of New-Amsterdam. It is generally supposed that he was the inventor of those excellent and respectable articles. However this may be, he lived and prospered in the little Dutch house in William-street called, time out of mind, Knickerbocker Hall, just at the outskirts of the good town of New-Amsterdam.

Boomptie was a fat comfortable creature, with a capital pair of oldfashioned legs; a full, round, good-natured face; a corporation like unto one of his plump loaves; and as much honesty as a Turkish baker, who lives in the fear of having his ears nailed to his own door for retailing bad bread. He wore a low-crowned, broad-brimmed beaver, a gray bearskin cloth coat, waistcoat, and breeches, and gray woollen stockings, summer and winter, all the year round. The only language he spoke, understood, or had the least respect for, was Dutch—and the only books he ever read or owned were a Dutch Bible, with silver clasps and hinges, and a Dutch history of the Duke of Alva's bloody wars in the Low Countries. Boss Boomptie was a pious man, of simple habits and simple character; a believer in "demonology and witchcraft"; and as much afraid of *spooks* as the mother that bore him. It ran in the family to be bewitched, and for three generations the Boompties had been very much pestered with supernatural visitations. But for all this they continued to prosper in the world, insomuch that Boss Boomptie daily added a piece of wampum or two to his strong box. He was blessed with a good wife, who saved the very parings of her nails, and three plump boys, after whom he modelled his gingerbread babies, and who were every Sunday zealously instructed never to pass a pin without picking it up and bringing it home to their mother.

It was on Newyear's eve, in the year 1655, and the good city of New-Amsterdam, then under the special patronage of the blessed St. Nicholas, was as jovial and wanton as hot spiced rum and long abstinence from fun and frolic could make it. It is worth while to live soberly and mind our business all the rest of the year, if it be only to enjoy the holydays at the end with a true zest. St. Nicholas, thrice blessed soul! was riding up one chimney and down another like a locomotive engine in his little one-horse wagon, distributing cakes to the good boys, and whips to the bad ones; and the laugh of the good city, which had been pent up all the year, now burst forth with an explosion that echoed even unto Breuckelen and Communipaw.

Boss Boomptie, who never forgot the main chance, and knew from experience that Newyear's eve was a shrewd time for selling cakes, joined profit and pleasure on this occasion. He was one minute in his shop, dealing out cakes to his customers, and the next laughing and tippling and jiggling and frisking it with his wife and children in the little back room, the door of which had a pane of glass that commanded a full view of the shop. Nobody—that is, no genuine disciple of jolly St. Nicholas—ever went to bed till twelve o'clock on Newyear's eve. The Dutch are eminently a sober, discreet folk; but somehow or other, no people frolic so like the very dickens, when they are once let loose, as your very sober and discreet bodies.

By twelve o'clock the spicy beverage, sacred to holydays at that time, began to mount up into Boss Boomptie's head, and he was vociferating a Dutch ditty in praise of St. Nicholas with marvellous discordance, when just as the old clock in one corner of the room struck the hour that ushers in the new year, a loud knock was heard on the counter, which roused the dormant spirit of trade within his bosom. He went into the shop, where he found a little ugly old thing of a woman, with a sharp chin, resting on a crooked black stick which had been burned in the fire and then polished; two high sharp cheek bones; two sharp black eyes; skinny lips; and a most diabolical pair of leather spectacles on a nose ten times sharper than her chin.

"I want a dozen Newyear cookies," screamed she, in a voice sharper than her nose.

"Vel, den, you needn't sbeak so loud," replied Boss Boomptie, whose ear being just then attuned to the melody of his own song, was somewhat outraged by this shrill salutation.

"I want a dozen Newyear cookies," screamed she again, ten times louder and shriller than ever.

"Duyvel—I an't teaf den," grumbled the worthy man, as he proceeded to count out the cakes, which the other very deliberately counted after him.

"I want a dozen," screamed the little woman; "here is only twelve."

"Vel, den, and what de duyvel is dwalf but a dozen?" said Boomptie.

"I tell you I want one more," screamed she, in a voice that roused Mrs. Boomptie in the back room, who came and peeped through the pane of glass, as she often did when she heard the boss talking to the ladies.

Boss Boomptie waxed wroth, for he had a reasonable quantity of hot spiced rum in his noddle, which predisposes a man to valour.

"Vel, den," said he, "you may co to de duyvel and get anoder, for you won't get it here."

Boomptie was not a stingy man; on the contrary, he was very generous to the pretty young damsels who came to buy cakes, and often gave them two or three extra for a smack, which made Mrs. Boomptie peevish sometimes, and caused her to watch at the little pane of glass when she ought to have been minding her business like an honest woman.

But this old hag was as ugly as sin, and the little baker never in his whole life could find in his heart to be generous to an ugly woman, old or young.

"In my country they always give thirteen to the

dozen," screamed the ugly woman in the leather spectacles.

"And where de duyvel is your gountry?" asked Boomptie.

"It is nobody's business," screeched the old woman. "But will you give me another cake, once for all?"

"Not if it would save me and all my chineration from peing pewitched and pedemonologized dime out of mind," cried he, in a great passion.

What put it into his head to talk in this way I don't know, but he might better have held his tongue. The old woman gave him three stivers for his cakes, and went away, grumbling something about "living to repent it," which Boss Boomptie didn't understand or care a fig about. He was chock full of Dutch courage, and defied all the ugly old women in Christendom. He put his three stivers in the till and shut up his shop, determined to enjoy the rest of the night without further molestation.

While he was sitting smoking his pipe, and now and then sipping his beverage, all at once he heard a terrible jingling of money in his shop, whereupon he thought some losel caitiff was busy with his little till. Accordingly, priming himself with another reinforcement of Dutch courage, he took a pine knot, for he was too economical to burn candles at that late hour, and proceeded to investigate. His money was all safe, and the till appeared not to have been disturbed.

"Duyvel," quoth the little baker man, "I pelieve mine *vrouw* and I have bote cot a zinging in our heads."

He had hardly turned his back when the same jingling began again, so much to the surprise of Boss Boomptie that, had it not been for his invincible Dutch courage, he would, as it were, have been a little frightened. But he was not in the least; and again went and unlocked the till, when what was his astonishment to see the three diabolical stivers, received from the old woman, dancing and kicking up a dust among the coppers and wampum with wonderful agility.

"*Wat donder is dat!*" exclaimed he, sorely perplexed; "de old duyvel has cot indo dat old sinner's stivers, I dink." He had a great mind to throw them away, but he thought it a pity to waste so much money; so he kept them locked up all night, enjoining them to good behaviour, with a design to spend them the next day in another jollification. But the next day they were gone, and so was the broomstick with which it was the custom to sweep out the shop every morning. Some of the neighbours coming home late the night before, on being informed of the "abduction" of the broomstick, deposed and said, they had seen an old woman riding through the air upon just such another, right over the top of the little bakehouse; whereat Boss Boomptie, putting these odds and ends together, did tremble in his heart, and he wished to himself that he had given the ugly old woman thirteen to the dozen.

Nothing particular came to pass the next day, except that now and then the little Boompties complained of having pins stuck in their backs, and that their cookies were snatched away by some one unknown. On examination it was found that no marks of the pins were to be seen; and as to the cookies, the old black woman of the kitchen declared she saw an invisible hand just as one of the children lost his commodity.

"Den I am pewitched, zure enough!" cried Boomptie, in despair, for he had had too much of "demonology and witchcraft" in the family not to know when he saw them, just as well as he did his own face in the Collect.

On the second day of the year, the 'prentice boys all returned to their business, and Boomptie once more solaced himself with the baking of the staff of life. The reader must know that it is the custom of bakers to knead a great batch at a time, in a mighty bread tray, into which they throw two or three little apprentice boys to paddle about like ducks in a mill pond, whereby it is speedily amalgamated, and set to rising in due time. When the little caitiffs began their gambols in this matter they one and all stuck fast in the dough, as though it had been so much pitch, and, to the utter dismay of honest Boomptie, behold! the whole batch rose up in a mighty mass, with the boys sticking fast on the top of it!

"Wat blikslager!" exclaimed little Boomptie, as he witnessed this catastrophe; "de duyvel ish cot into de yeast dis dime, I dink."

The bread continued to rise till it lifted the roof off the bakehouse, with the little 'prentice boys on the top, and the bread tray following after. Boss Boomptie and his wife watched this wonderful rising of the bread in dismay, and in proof of the poor woman's being bewitched, it was afterwards recollected that she uttered not a single word on this extraordinary occasion. The bread rose and rose, until it finally disappeared, boys and all, behind the Jersey hills. If such things had been known of at that time, it would have been taken for a balloon; as it was, the people of Bergen and Communipaw thought that it was a water spout.

Little Boss Boomptie was disconsolate at the loss of his bread and his 'prentice boys, whom he never expected to see again. However, he was a stirring body, and set himself to work to prepare another batch, seeing his customers must be supplied in spite of "witchcraft or demonology." To guard against such another rebellious rising, he determined to go through the process down in the cellar, and turn his bread tray upside down. The bread, instead of rising, began to sink into the earth so fast that Boss Boomptie had just time to jump off before it entirely disappeared in the ground, which opened and shut just like a snuffbox.

"Wat blikslager is dat!" exclaimed he, out of breath; "my pread rises downward dis dime, I dink. My customers must go widout to-day."

By-and-by his customers came for hot rolls and muffins, but some of them had gone up and some down, as little Boss Boomptie related after the manner just described. What is very remarkable, nobody believed him; and doubtless, if there had been any rival baker in New-Amsterdam, the boss would have lost all his customers. Among those that called on this occasion, was the ugly old woman with the sharp eyes, nose, chin, voice, and leather spectacles.

"I want a dozen Newyear cookies!" screamed she, as before.

"Vuur en vlammen!" muttered he, as he counted out the twelve cakes.

"I want one more!" screamed she.

"Den you may co do de duyvel and kit it, I say, for not anoder shall you haf here, I dell you."

So the old woman took her twelve cakes, and went out grumbling, as before. All the time she staid, Boomptie's old dog, who followed him wherever he went, growled and whined, as it were, to himself, and seemed mightily relieved when she went away. That very night, as the little baker was going to see one of his old neighbours at the *Maiden's Valley,* then a little way out of town, walking, as he always did, with his hands behind him, every now and then he felt something as cold as death against them, which he could never account for, seeing there was not a soul with him but his old dog. Moreover, Mrs. Boomptie, having bought half a pound of tea at a grocery store, and put it into her pocket, did feel a twitching and jerking of the paper of tea in her pocket, every step she went. The faster she ran the quicker and stronger was the twitching and jerking, so that when the good woman got home she was nigh fainting away. On her recovery she took courage, and pulled the tea out of her pocket, and laid it on the table, when behold it began to move by fits and starts, jumped off the table, hopped out of doors, all alone by itself, and jigged away to the place from whence it came. The grocer brought it back again, but Madam Boomptie looked upon the whole as a judgment for her extravagance in laying out so much money for tea, and refused to receive it again. The grocer assured her that the strange capers of the bundle were owing to his having forgot to cut the twine with which he had tied it; but the good woman looked upon this as an ingenious subterfuge, and would take nothing but her money. When the husband and wife came to compare notes, they both agreed they were certainly bewitched. Had there been any doubt of the matter, subsequent events would soon have put it to rest.

That very night Mrs. Boomptie was taken after a strange way. Sometimes she would laugh about nothing, and then she would cry about nothing; then she would set to work and talk about nothing for a whole hour without stopping, in a language nobody could understand; and then, all at once, her tongue would cleave to the roof of her mouth, so that it was impossible to force it away. When this fit was over she would get up and dance double trouble, till she tired herself out, when she fell asleep, and waked up quite rational. It was particularly noticed that when she talked loudest and fastest, her lips remained perfectly closed, without motion, and her mouth wide open, so that words seemed to come from down her throat. Her principal talk was railing against Dominie Laidlie, the good pastor of Garden-street Church, whence everybody concluded that she was possessed by a devil. Sometimes she got hold of a pen, and though she had never learned to write, would scratch and scrawl certain mysterious and diabolical figures that nobody could understand, and everybody said must mean something.

As for little Boss Boomptie, he was worse off than his wife. He was haunted by an invisible hand, which played him all sorts of scurvy tricks. Standing one morning at his counter, talking to one of the neighbours, he received a great box on the ear, whereat being exceeding wroth, he returned it with such interest on the cheek of his neighbour that he laid him flat on the floor. His friend hereupon took the law of him, and proved, to the satisfaction of the court, that he had both hands in his breeches pockets at the time Boss Boomptie said he gave him the box on the ear. The magistrate not being able to come at the truth of the matter, fined them each twenty-five guilders for the use of the dominie.

A dried codfish was one day thrown at his head, and the next minute his walking stick fell to beating him, though nobody seemed to have hold of it. A chair danced about the room, and at last alighted on the dinner table, and began to eat with such a good appetite that had not the children snatched some of the dinner away, there would have been none left. The old cow one night jumped over the moon, and a pewter dish ran fairly off with a horn spoon, which seized a cat by the tail, and away they all went together, as merry as crickets. Sometimes, when Boss Boomptie had money, or cakes, or perhaps a loaf of bread in his hand, instead of putting them in their proper places he would throw them into the fire, in spite of his teeth, and then the invisible hand would beat him with a bag of flour, till he was as white as a miller. As for keeping his accounts, that was out of the question; whenever he sat himself down to write, his ink horn was snatched away by the invisible hand, and by-and-by it would come tumbling down the chimney. Sometimes an old dishcloth would be pinned to the skirt of his coat, and then a great diabolical laugh heard under the floor. At night he had a pretty time of it. His nightcap was torn off his head, his hair pulled out by handfuls, his face scratched, and his ears pinched as if with a red-hot pincers. If he went out in the yard at night, he was pelted with brickbats, sticks, stones, and all sorts of filthy missives; and if he staid at home, the ashes were blown upon his supper; and old shoes, instead of plates, seen on the table. One of the frying pans rang every night of itself for a whole hour, and a three-pronged fork stuck itself voluntarily into Boss Boomptie's back, without hurting him in the least. But what astonished the neighbours more than all, the little man, all at once, took to speaking in a barbarous and unknown jargon, which was afterwards found out to be English.

These matters frightened some of the neighbours and scandalized others, until at length poor Boomptie's shop was almost deserted. People were jealous of eating his bread, for fear of being bewitched. Nay, more than one little urchin complained grievously of horrible, out-of-the-way pains in the stomach, after eating two or three dozen of his Newyear cookies.

Things went on in this way until Newyear's eve came round again, when Boss Boomptie was sitting behind his counter, which was wont to be thronged with customers on this occasion, but was now quite deserted. While thinking on his present miserable state and future prospects, all of a sudden the little ugly old woman, with a sharp nose, sharp chin, sharp eyes, sharp voice, and leather spectacles, again stood before him, leaning on her crooked black cane.

"Ben je bedondered?" exclaimed Boss Boomptie, "what to you want now?"

"I want a dozen Newyear cookies!" screamed the old creature.

The little man counted out twelve, as before.

"I want one more!" screamed she, louder than ever.

"Men weet hoe een koe een haas vangen kan!" cried the boss, in a rage; "den want will pe your masder."

She offered him six stivers, which he indignantly rejected, saying,

"I want none of your duyvel's stuyvers—begone, duyvel's huysvrouw!"

The old woman went her way, mumbling and grumbling as usual.

"By St. Johannes de Dooper," quoth Boss Boomptie, "put she's a peaudy!"

That night, and all the week after, the brickbats flew about Knickerbocker Hall like hail, insomuch that Boss Boomptie marveled where they could all come from, until one morning, after a terrible shower of bricks, he found to his great grief and dismay that his oven had disappeared; next went the top of his chimney; and when that was gone, these diabolical sinners began at the extreme point of the gable end, and so went on picking at the two edges downward, until they looked just like the teeth of a saw, as may be still seen in some of our old Dutch houses.

"Onbegrypelik!" cried Boss Boomptie, "put it's too pad to have my prains peat out wid my own prickpats."

About the same time a sober respectable cat, that for years had done nothing but sit purring in the chimney corner, all at once got the duyvel in her, and after scratching the poor man half to death, jumped out of the chimney and disappeared. A Whitehall boatman afterwards saw her in Buttermilk Channel, with nothing but the tail left, swimming against the tide as easy as kiss your hand. Poor Mrs. Boomptie had no peace of her life, what with pinchings, stickings of needles, and talking without opening her mouth. But the climax of the malice of the demon which beset her was in at last tying up her tongue, so that she could not speak at all, but did nothing but sit crying and wringing her hands in the chimney corner.

These carryings-on brought round Newyear's eve again, when Boss Boomptie thought he would have a frolic, "in spite of de duyvel," as he said, which saying was, somehow or other, afterwards applied to the creek at Kingsbridge. So he commanded his wife to prepare him a swinging mug of hot spiced rum, to keep up his courage against the assaults of the brickbats. But what was the dismay of the little man when he found that every time he put the beverage to his lips he received a great box on the ear, the mug was snatched away by an invisible hand, and every single drop drank out of it before it came to Boss Boomptie's turn. Then as if it was an excellent joke, he heard a most diabolical laugh down in the cellar.

"Goeden Hemel! Is het mogelyk!" exclaimed the little man in despair. This was attacking him in the very intrenchments of his heart. It was worse than the brickbats.

"St. Nicholas! St. Nicholas! what will become of me—what sal ich doon, mynheer?"

Scarcely had he uttered this pathetic appeal, when there was a sound of horses' hoofs in the chimney, and presently a light wagon, drawn by a little, fat, gray 'Sopus pony, came trundling into the room, loaded with all sorts of knickknacks. It was driven by a jolly, fat, little rogue of a fellow, with a round sparkling eye, and a mouth which would certainly have been laughing had it not been for a glorious meershaum pipe, which would have chanced to fall out in that case. The little rascal had on a three-cornered cocked hat, decked with old gold lace, a blue Dutch sort of a short pea jacket, red waistcoat, breeks of the same colour, yellow stockings, and honest thick-soled shoes, ornamented with a pair of skates. Altogether he was a queer figure—but there was something so irresistibly jolly and good-natured in his face, that Boss Boomptie felt his heart incline towards the stranger as soon as he saw him.

"Orange Boven!" cried the good saint, pulling off his cocked hat, and making a low bow to Mrs. Boomptie, who sat tonguetied in the chimney corner.

"Wad donderdag is dat?" said Boss Boomptie, speaking for his wife, which made the good woman very angry, that he should take the words out of her mouth.

"You called on St. Nicholas. Here am I," quoth the jolly little saint. "In one word—for I am a saint of few words, and have my hands full of business to-night—in one word, tell me what you want."

"I am pewitched," quoth Boss Boomptie. "The

duyvel is in me, my house, my wife, my Newyear cookies, and my children. What shall I do?"

"When you count a dozen you must count thirteen," answered the wagon driver, at the same time cracking his whip, and clattering up the chimney, more like a little duyvel than a little saint.

"Wat blixum!" muttered Boss Boomptie, "when you count a dozen you must count dirdeen! je mag even wel met un stokje in de goot roeron! I never heard of such counting. By St. Johannes de Dooper, put St. Nicholas is a great plockhead!"

Just as he uttered this blasphemy against the excellent St. Nicholas, he saw through the pane of glass, in the door leading from the spare room to the shop, the little ugly old woman with the sharp eyes, sharp nose, sharp chin, sharp voice, and leather spectacles, alighting from a broomstick at the street door.

"Dere is de duyvel's kint come again," quoth he, in one of his cross humours, which was aggravated by his getting just then a great box on the ear from the invisible hand. However, he went grumbling into the shop, for it was part of his religion never to neglect a customer, let the occasion be what it might.

"I want a dozen Newyear cookies," screamed the

old beauty, as usual, and as usual Boss Boomptie counted out twelve.

"I want another one," screamed she still louder.

"Aha!" thought Boss Boomptie, doubtless inspired by the jolly little caitiff, St. Nicholas—"Aha! Het is goed visschen in troebel water—when you count dwalf, you must count dirdeen. Ha—ha! ho—ho—ho!" And he counted out the thirteenth cooky like a brave fellow.

The old woman made him a low courtesy, and laughed till she might have shown her teeth, if she had had any.

"Friend Boomptie," said she, in a voice exhibiting the perfection of a nicely modulated scream— "Friend Boomptie, I love such generous little fellows as you, in my heart. I salute you," and she advanced to kiss him. Boss Boomptie did not at all like the proposition; but, doubtless inspired by St. Nicholas, he submitted with indescribable grace.

At that moment, an explosion was heard inside the little glass pane, and the voice of Mrs. Boomptie crying out,

"You false-hearted villain, have I found out your tricks at last!"

"De Philistyner Onweetende!" cried Boss Boomptie. "She's come to her speech now!"

"The spell is broken!" screamed the old woman with the sharp eyes, nose, chin, and voice. "The spell is broken, and henceforward a dozen is thirteen, and thirteen is a dozen! There shall be thirteen Newyear cookies to the dozen, as a type of the thirteen mighty states that are to arise out of the ruins of the government of faderland!"

Thereupon she took a Newyear cake bearing the effigy of the blessed St. Nicholas, and caused Boss Boomptie to swear upon it that for ever afterwards twelve should be thirteen, and thirteen should be twelve. After which, she mounted her broomstick and disappeared, just as the little old Dutch clock struck twelve. From that time forward, the spell that hung over the fortunes of little Boss Boomptie was broken; and ever after he became illustrious for baking the most glorious Newyear cookies in our country. Everything became as before: the little 'prentice boys returned, mounted on the batch of bread, and their adventures may, peradventure, be told some other time. Finally, from that day forward no baker of New-Amsterdam was ever bewitched, at least by an ugly old woman, and a baker's dozen has been always counted as thirteen.

THE

Ride of Saint Nicholas
on Newyear's Eve

Of all the cities in this New World, that which once bore the name of Fort Orange, but now bears it no more, is the favourite of the good St. Nicholas. It is there that he hears the sound of his native language, and sees the honest Dutch pipe in the mouths of a few portly burghers, who, disdaining the pestilent innovations of modern times, still cling with honest obstinacy to the dress, the manners, and customs of old faderland. It is there, too, that they have instituted a society in honour of the excellent saint, whose birthday they celebrate in a manner worthy of all commendation.

True it is, that the city of his affections has from time to time committed divers great offences, which sorely wounded the feelings of St. Nicholas, and almost caused him to withdraw his patronage from its backsliding citizens. First, by adopting the newfangled style of beginning the year at the bidding of the old lady of Babylon, whereby the jolly Newyear was so jostled out of place that the good saint scarcely knew where to look for it. Next, they essayed themselves to learn outlandish tongues, whereby they gradually sophisticated their own, insomuch that he could hardly understand them. Thirdly, they did, from time to time, admit into their churches preachings and singings in the upstart English language, until by degrees the ancient worship became adulterated in such a manner that the indignant St. Nicholas, when he first witnessed it, did for the only time in his life come near to uttering a great oath, by exclaiming, "Wat donderdag is dat?" Now be it known that had he said, "Wat donder is dat," it would have been downright swearing; so you see what a narrow escape he had.

Not content with these backslidings, the burghers of Fort Orange—a pestilence on all new names! —suffered themselves by degrees to be corrupted by various modern innovations, under the mischievous disguise of improvements. Forgetting the reverence due to their ancestors, who eschewed all internal improvement except that of the mind and heart, they

departed from the venerable customs of the faderland, and pulling down the old houses that, scorning
all appearance of ostentation, modestly presented the
little end to the street, began to erect in their places
certain indescribable buildings with the broadsides as
it were turned frontwise, by which strange contortion
the comeliness of Fort Orange was utterly destroyed.
It is on record that a heavy judgment fell upon the
head of the first man who adventured on this daring
innovation. His money gave out before this mon-
strous novelty was completed, and he invented the
pernicious system of borrowing and mortgaging, before happily unknown among these worthy citizens,
who were utterly confounded, not long afterwards, at
seeing the house change its owner—a thing that had
never happened before in that goodly community,
save when the son entered on the inheritance of his
father.

Becoming gradually more incorrigible in their
backslidings, they were seduced into opening, widening, and regulating the streets; making the
crooked straight and the narrow wide, thereby caus-
ing sad inroads into the strong boxes of divers of the
honest burghers, who became all at once very rich,
saving that they had no money to go to market.
To cap the climax of their enormities, they at last

committed the egregious sacrilege of pulling down the ancient and honourable Dutch church, which stood right in the middle of State-street, or Staats-street, being so called after the family of that name, from which I am lineally descended.

At this the good St. Nicholas was exceedingly grieved; and when, by degrees, his favourite burghers left off eating sturgeon, being thereto instigated by divers scurvy jests of certain silly strangers, that knew not the excellence of that savoury fish, he cried out in the bitterness of his soul, *"Onbegrypelyk!"*— "Incredible!"—meaning thereby that he could scarely believe his eyes. In the bitterness of his soul he had resolved to return to faderland, and leave his beloved city to be swallowed up in the vortex of improvement. He was making his progress through the streets, to take his last farewell, in melancholy mood, when he came to the outlet of the Grand Canal, just then completed. *"Is het mogelyk?"*— which means, "Is it possible?"—exclaimed St. Nicholas; and thereupon he was so delighted with this proof that his beloved people had not altogether degenerated from their ancestors, that he determined not to leave them to strange saints, outlandish tongues, and modern innovations. He took a sail on the canal, and returned in such measureless content that he blessed the good city of Fort Orange, as he evermore called it, and resolved to distribute a more than usual store of his Newyear cookies, at the Christmas holydays. That jovial season was now fast approaching. The autumn frosts had already invested the forests with a mantle of glory; the farmers were in their fields and orchards, gathering in the corn and apples, or making cider, the wholesome beverage of virtuous simplicity; the robins, blackbirds, and all the annual emigrants to southern climes, had passed away in flocks, like the adventurers to the far West; the bluebird alone lingered last of all to sing his parting song; and sometimes of a morning, the river showed a little fretted border of ice, looking like a fringe of lace on the garment of some decayed dowager. At length the liquid glass of the river cooled into a wide, immoveable mirror, glistening in the sun; the trees, all save the evergreens, stood bare to the keen cold winds; the fields were covered with snow, affording no lures to tempt to rural wanderings; the enjoyments of life gradually centred themselves at the cheerful fireside—it was winter, and Newyear's eve was come again!

The night was clear, calm, and cold, and the bright stars glittered in the heavens in such multitudes that every man might have had a star to himself. The worthy patriarchs of Fort Orange, having gathered around them their children, and children's children, even unto the third and fourth generation, were enjoying themselves in innocent revelry at the cheerful fireside. All the enjoyments of life had contracted themselves into the domestic circle; the streets were as quiet as a churchyard, and not even the stroke of the watchman was heard on the curbstone. Gradually it waxed late, and the city clocks rang, in the silence of night, the hour which not one of the orderly citizens had heard, except at midday, since the last anniversary of the happy Newyear, save peradventure troubled with a toothache, or some such unseemly irritation.

The doleful warning which broke upon the frosty air like the tolling of a funeral bell, roused the sober devotees of St. Nicholas to a sense of their trespasses on the waning night, and after one good, smoking draught of spiced Jamaica to the patron saint, they, one and all, young and old, hied them to bed, that he might have a fair opportunity to bestow his favours without being seen by mortal eye. For be it known that St. Nicholas, like all really heart-whole generous fellows, loves to do good in secret, and eschews those pompous benefactions which are duly recorded in the newspapers, being of opinion they only prove that the vanity of man is sometimes an overmatch for his avarice.

Having allowed them fifteen minutes, which is as much as a sober burgher of good morals and habits requires to get as fast asleep as a church, St. Nicholas, having harnessed his pony and loaded his little wagon with a store of good things for well-behaved, diligent children, together with whips and other mementoes for undutiful varlets, did set forth gayly on his errand of benevolence.

Vuur en vlammen! how the good saint did hurry through the streets, up one chimney and down another; for be it known, they are not such miserable narrow things as those of other cities, where the claims of ostentation are so voracious that people can't afford to keep up good fires, and the chimneys are so narrow that the little sweeps of seven years old often get themselves stuck fast, to the imminent peril of their lives. You may think he had a good deal of business on hand, being obliged to visit every house in Fort Orange between twelve o'clock and daylight, with the exception of some few would-be fashionable upstarts, who had mortally offended him by turning up their noses at the simple jollifications and friendly greetings of the merry Newyear. Accordingly, he rides like the wind, scarcely touching the ground;

and this is the reason that he is never seen, except by a rare chance, which is the cause why certain unbelieving sinners, who scoff at old customs and notions, either really do, or pretend to doubt whether the good things found on Christmas and Newyear mornings in the stockings of the little varlets of Fort Orange and New-Amsterdam are put there by the jolly St. Nicholas or not. Beshrew them, say I—and may they never taste the blessing of his bounty! *Goeden Hemel!* as if I myself, being a kinsman of the saint, don't know him as well as a debtor does his creditor! But people are grown so wise nowadays, that they believe in nothing but the increased value of property.

Be this as it may, St. Nicholas went forth blithely on his goodly errand, without minding the intense cold, for he was kept right warm by the benevolence of his heart, and when that failed, he ever and anon addressed himself to a snug little pottle, the contents of which did smoke lustily when he pulled out the stopper, a piece of snow-white corn cob.

It is impossible for me to specify one by one the visits paid that night by the good saint, or the various adventures which he encountered. I therefore content myself, and I trust my worthy and excellent readers, with dwelling briefly on those which appear to me most worthy of descending to posterity, and withal convey excellent moral lessons, without which history is naught, whether it be true or false.

After visiting various honest little Dutch houses, with notched roofs and the gable ends to the street, leaving his benedictions, St. Nicholas at length came to a goodly mansion bearing strong marks of being sophisticated by modern fantastic innovations. He would have passed it by in scorn, had he not remembered that it belonged to a descendant of one of his favoured votaries, who had passed away to his long home without being once backslided from the customs of his ancestors. Respect for the memory of this worthy man wrought upon his feelings, and he forthwith dashed down the chimney, where he stuck fast in the middle, and came nigh being suffocated with the fumes of anthracite coal, which this degenerate descendant of a pious ancestor, who spent thousands in useless and unseemly ostentation, burned by way of economy.

If the excellent saint had not been enveloped, as it were, in the odour of sanctity, which in some measure protected him from the poison of this pestilent vapour, it might have gone hard with him; as it was, he was sadly bewildered, when his little pony, which liked the predicament no better than his master, made a violent plunge, drew the wagon through the narrow passage, and down they came plump into a magnificent bedchamber, filled with all sorts of finery, such as wardrobes bedizened with tawdry ornaments; satin chairs too good to be looked at or sat upon, and therefore covered with brown linen; a bedstead of varnished mahogany, with a canopy over it somewhat like a cocked hat, with a plume of ostrich feathers instead of orthodox valances and the like; and a looking-glass large enough to reflect a Dutch city.

St. Nicholas contemplated the pair who slept in this newfangled abomination with a mingled feeling of pity and indignation, though I must say the wife looked very pretty in her lace nightcap, with one arm as white as snow partly uncovered. But he soon turned away, being a devout and self-denying saint, to seek for the stockings of the little children, who were innocent of these unseemly innovations. But what was his horror at finding that, instead of being hung up in the chimney corner, they were thrown carelessly on the floor, and that the little souls, who lay asleep in each other's arms in another room lest they should disturb their parents, were thus deprived of all the pleasant anticipations accompanying the approaching jolly Newyear.

"Een vervlocte jonge," said he to himself, for he never uttered his maledictions aloud, "to rob their little ones of such wholesome and innocent delights! But they shall not be disappointed." So he sought the cold and distant chamber of the children, who were virtuous and dutiful, and who, when they waked in the morning, found the bed covered with good things, and were as happy as the day is long. Then St. Nicholas returned to the splendid chamber, which, be it known, was furnished with the spoils of industrious unfortunate people to whom the owner lent money, charging them so much the more in proportion to their necessities. It is true that he gave some of the wealth he thus got over the duyvel's back, as it were, to public charities and sometimes churches, when he knew it would get into the news-papers, by which he obtained the credit of being very pious and charitable. But St. Nicholas was too sensible and judicious not to know that the only charitable and pious donations agreeable to the Giver of good, are those which are honestly come by. The alms which are got by ill means can never come to good, and it is better to give back to those from whom we have taken it dishonestly even one fourth, yea, one tenth, than to bestow ten times as much on those who have no such claim. The true atonement for injuries is that made to the injured alone. All other is a cheat in the eye of Heaven. You cannot settle the account by giving to Peter what you have filched from Paul.

So thought the good St. Nicholas, as he revolved in his mind a plan for punishing this degenerate caitiff, who despised his ordinances and customs, and was moreover one who, in dealing with borrowers, not only shaved but skinned them. Remembering not the perils of the chimney, he was about to depart the same way he came, but the little pony obstinately refused; and the good saint, having first taken off the lace nightcap and put a foolscap in its place, and given the money lender a tweak of the nose that made him roar, whipped instantly through the keyhole to pursue his benevolent tour through the ancient city of Fort Orange.

Gliding through the streets unheard and unseen, he at length came to a little winding lane, from which his quick ear caught the sound of obstreperous revelry. Stopping his pony, and listening more attentively, he distinguished the words "Ich ben Lie-derich," roared out in a chorus of mingled voices seemingly issuing from a little low house of the true orthodox construction, standing on the right-hand side, at a distance of a hundred yards or thereabout.

"*Wat donderdag!*" exclaimed St. Nicholas, "is mine old friend, Baltus Van Loon, keeping it up at this time of the morning? The old rogue! but I'll punish him for this breach of the good customs of Fort Orange." So he halted on the top of Baltus's chimney, to consider the best way of bringing it about, and was, all at once, saluted in the nostrils by such a delectable perfume, arising from a certain spiced beverage with which the substantial burghers were wont to recreate themselves at this season of the year, that he was sorely tempted to join a little in the revelry below, and punish the merry caitiffs afterwards. Presently he heard honest Baltus propose— "The jolly St. Nicholas," as a toast, which was drunk in a full bumper, with great rejoicing and acclamation.

St. Nicholas could stand it no longer, but descended forthwith into the little parlour of old Baltus, thinking, by-the-way, that, just to preserve appearances, he would lecture the roistering rogues a little for keeping such late hours, and, provided Baltus could give a good reason, or indeed any reason at all, for such an unseemly transgression, he would then sit down with them, and take some of the savoury beverage that had regaled his nostrils while waiting at the top of the chimney.

The roistering rogues were so busy roaring out "Ich ben Liederich" that they did not take note of the presence of the saint, until he cried out with a loud and angry voice, "Wat blikslager is dat?"—he did not say blixem, because that would have been little better than swearing. "Ben je be dondered, to be carousing here at this time of night, ye ancient, and not venerable sinners?"

Old Baltus was not a little startled at the intrusion of the strangers—for, if the truth must out, he was a little in for it, and saw double, as is usual at such times. This caused such a confusion in his head that he forgot to rise from his seat, and pay due honour to his visitor, as did the rest of the company.

"Are you not ashamed of yourselves," continued the saint, "to set such a bad example to the neighbourhood, by carousing at this time of the morning, contrary to good old customs, known and accepted by all, except such noisy splutterkins as yourselves?"

"This time of the morning," replied old Baltus, who had his full portion of Dutch courage—"this time of the morning, did you say? Look yonder, and

see with your own eyes whether it is morning or
not."

The cunning rogue, in order to have a good excuse for transgressing the canons of St. Nicholas, had
so managed it that the old clock in the corner had
run down, and now pointed to the hour of eleven,
where it remained stationary, like a rusty weathercock. St. Nicholas knew this as well as old Baltus
himself, and could not help being mightily tickled
at this device. He told Baltus that this being the
case, with permission of his host he would sit down
by the fire and warm himself, till it was time to set
forth again, seeing he had mistaken the hour.

Baltus, who by this time began to perceive that
there was but one visitor instead of two, now rose
from the table with much ado, and approaching the
stranger, besought him to take a seat among the jolly
revellers, seeing they were there assembled in honour
of St. Nicholas, and not out of any regard to the lusts
of the flesh. In this he was joined by the rest of the
company, so that St. Nicholas, being a good-natured
fellow, at length suffered himself to be persuaded,
whereto he was mightily incited by the savoury
fumes issuing from a huge pitcher standing smoking
in the chimney corner. So he sat down with old Bal-

tus, and being called on for a toast, gave them "Old Faderland" in a bumper.

Then they had a high time of it you may be sure. Old Baltus sang a famous song celebrating the valour of our Dutch ancestors, and their triumph over the mighty power of Spain after a struggle of more than a generation, in which the meads of Holland smoked and her canals were red with blood. *Goeden Hemel!* but I should like to have been there, for I hope it would have been nothing unseemly for one of my cloth to have joined in chorus with the excellent St. Nicholas. Then they talked about the good old times when the son who departed from the customs of his ancestors was considered little better than misbegotten; lamented over the interloping of such multitudes of idle flaunting men and women in their way to and from the springs; the increase of taverns, the high price of everything, and the manifold backslidings of the rising generation. Ever and anon, old Baltus would observe that sorrow was as dry as a corn cob, and pour out a full bumper of the smoking beverage, until at last it came to pass that honest Baltus and his worthy companions, being not used to such late hours, fell fast asleep in their goodly armchairs, and snored lustily in concert. Whereupon St. Nicholas, feeling a little waggish, after putting their wigs the hinder part before and placing a great China bowl upside down on the head of old Baltus, who sat nodding like a mandarin, departed laughing ready to split his sides. In the morning, when Baltus and his companions awoke and saw what a figure they cut, they laid all the trick to the door of the stranger, and never knew to the last day of their lives who it was that caroused with them so lustily on Newyear's morning.

Pursuing his way in high good humour, being somewhat exhilarated by the stout carousal with old Baltus and his roistering companions, St. Nicholas in good time came into the ancient *Colonie,* which being, as it were, at the outskirts of Fort Orange, was inhabited by many people not well-to-do in the world. He descended the chimney of an old weatherworn house that bore evident marks of poverty, for he is not one of those saints that hanker after palaces and turn their backs on their friends. It is his pleasure to seek out and administer to the innocent gratifications of those who are obliged to labour all the year round, and can only spare time to be merry at Christmas and Newyear. He is indeed the poor man's saint.

On entering the room, he was struck with the appearance of poverty and desolation that reigned all around. A number of little children of different ages, but none more than ten years old, lay huddled close together on a straw bed which was on the floor, their limbs intertwined to keep themselves warm, for their covering was scant and miserable. Yet they slept in peace, for they had quiet countenances, and hunger seeks refuge in the oblivion of repose. In a corner of the room stood a miserable bed, on which lay a female whose face, as the moonbeams fell upon it through a window without shutters, many panes of which were stuffed with old rags to keep out the nipping air of the winter night, bore evidence of long and painful suffering. It looked like death rather than sleep. A little pine table, a few broken chairs, and a dresser, whose shelves were ill supplied, constituted the remainder of the furniture of this mansion of poverty.

As he stood contemplating the scene, his honest old heart swelled with sorrowful compassion, saying to himself, "God bewaar ous, but this is pitiful." At that moment, a little child on the straw bed cried out in a weak voice that went to the heart of the saint, "Mother, mother, give me to eat—I am hungry." St. Nicholas went to the child, but she was fast asleep, and hunger had infected her very dreams. The mother did not hear, for long-continued sorrow and suffering sleep sounder than happiness, as the waters lie stillest when the tempest is past.

Again the little child cried out, "Mother, mother, I am freezing—give me some more covering." "Be quiet, Blandina," answered a voice deep and hoarse, yet not unkind; and St. Nicholas, looking around to see whence it came, beheld a man sitting close in the chimney corner, though there was no fire burning, his arms folded close around him, and his head drooping on his bosom. He was clad like one of the children of poverty, and his teeth chattered with cold. St. Nicholas wiped his eyes, for he was a good-hearted saint, and coming close up to the miserable man, said to him kindly, "How do ye, my good friend?"

"Friend," said the other, "I have no friend but God, and he seems to have deserted me." As he said this, he raised his saddened eyes to the good saint, and after looking at him a little while, as if he was not conscious of his presence, dropped them again, even without asking who he was, or whence he came, or what he wanted. Despair had deadened his faculties, and nothing remained in his mind but the consciousness of suffering.

"*Het is jammer, het is jammer*—it is a pity, it is a

pity!" quoth the kind-hearted saint, as he passed his sleeve across his eyes. "But something must be done, and that quickly too." So he shook the poor man somewhat roughly by the shoulder, and cried out, "Ho! ho! what aileth thee, son of my good old friend, honest Johannes Garrebrantze?"

This salutation seemed to rouse the poor man, who arose upon his seat, and essaying to stand upright, fell into the arms of St. Nicholas, who almost believed it was a lump of ice, so cold and stiff did it seem. Now, be it known that Providence, as a reward for his benevolent disposition, has bestowed on St. Nicholas the privilege of doing good without measure to all who are deserving of his bounty, and that by such means as he thinks proper to the purpose. It is a power he seldom exerts to the uttermost, except on pressing occasions, and this he believed one of them.

Perceiving that the poor man was wellnigh frozen to death, he called into action the supernatural faculties which had been committed to him, and lo! in an instant a rousing fire blazed on the hearth, towards which the poor man, instinctively as it were, edged his chair, and stretched out one of his bony hands, that was as stiff as an icicle. The light flashed so brightly in the face of the little ones and their mother that they awoke, and seeing the cheerful blaze, arose in their miserable clothing, which they had worn to aid in keeping them warm, and hied as fast as they could to bask in its blessed warmth. So eager were they that for a while they were unconscious of the presence of a stranger, although St. Nicholas had now assumed his proper person, that he might not be taken for some one of those diabolical wizards who, being always in mischief, are ashamed to show their faces among honest people.

At length the poor man, who was called after his father Johannes Garrebrantze, being somewhat revived by the genial warmth of the fire, looked around, and became aware of the presence of the stranger, which inspired him with a secret awe for which he could not account, insomuch that his voice trembled, though now he was not cold, when after some hesitation he said,

"Stranger, thou art welcome to this poor house. I would I were better able to offer thee the hospitalities of the season, but I will wish thee a happy New-year, and that is all I can bestow." The good yffrouw, his wife, repeated the wish, and straightway began to apologize for the untidy state of her apartment.

"Make no apologies," replied the excellent saint; "I come to give, not to receive. To-night I treat, to-morrow you may return the kindness to others."

"I?" said Johannes Garrebrantze; "I have nothing to bestow but good wishes, and nothing to receive but the scorn and neglect of the world. If I had anything to give thee to eat or drink, thou shouldst have it with all my heart. But the new year, which brings jollity to the hearts of others, brings nothing but hunger and despair to me and mine."

"Thou hast seen better days, I warrant thee," answered the saint; "for thou speakest like a scholar of Leyden. Tell me thy story, Johannes, my son, and we shall see whether in good time thou wilt not hold up thy head as high as a church steeple."

"Alas! to what purpose, since man assuredly has, and Heaven seems to have forsaken me."

"Hush!" cried St. Nicholas, "Heaven never forsakes the broken spirit, or turns a deaf ear to the cries of innocent children. It is for the wicked never to hope, the virtuous never to despair. I predict thou shalt live to see better days."

"I must see them soon then, for neither I, my wife, nor my children have tasted food since twenty-four hours past."

"What! God be with us! is there such lack of

charity in the burghers of the *Colonie,* that they will suffer a neighbour to starve under their very noses? *Onbegrypelik*—I'll not believe it."

"They know not my necessities."

"No? What! hast thou no tongue to speak them?"

"I am too proud to beg."

"And too lazy to work," cried St. Nicholas, in a severe tone.

"Look you," answered the other, holding up his right arm with his left, and showing that the sinews were stiffened by rheumatism.

"Is it so, my friend? Well, but thou mightst still have bent thy spirit to ask charity for thy starving wife and children, though, in truth, begging is the last thing an honest man ought to stoop to. But *Goeden Hemel!* here am I talking while thou and thine are perishing with hunger."

Saying which, St. Nicholas straightway bade the good yffrouw to bring forth the little pine table, which she did, making divers apologies for the want of a tablecloth; and when she had done so, he incontinently spread out upon it such store of good things from his little cart as made the hungry childrens' mouths to water, and smote the hearts of their parents with joyful thanksgivings. "Eat, drink, and be merry," said St. Nicholas, "for tomorrow thou shalt not die, but live."

The heart of the good saint expanded, like as the morning-glory does to the first rays of the sun, while he sat rubbing his hands at seeing them eat with such a zest as made him almost think it was worth while to be hungry in order to enjoy such triumphant satisfaction. When they had done, and returned their pious thanks to Heaven and the good stranger, St. Nicholas willed the honest man to expound the causes which had brought him to his present deplorable condition. "My own folly," said he; and the other sagely replied, "I thought as much. Beshrew me, friend, if in all my experience, and I have lived long, and seen much, I ever encountered distress and poverty that could not be traced to its source in folly or vice. Heaven is too bountiful to entail misery on its creatures, save through their own transgressions. But I pray thee, go on with thy story."

The good man then went on to relate that his father, old Johannes Garrebrantze—

"Ah!" quoth St. Nicholas, "I knew him well. He was an honest man, and that, in these times of all sorts of improvements, except in mind and morals, is little less than miraculous. But I interrupt thee, friend—proceed with thy story, once more."

The son of Johannes again resumed his story, and related how his father had left him a competent estate in the *Colonie,* on which he lived in good credit and in the enjoyment of a reasonable competency, with his wife and children, until within a few years past, when seeing a vast number of three-story houses with folding doors and marble mantelpieces rising up all around him, he began to be ashamed of his little one-story house with the gable end to the street, and—

"Ah! Johannes," interrupted the pale wife, "do not spare me. It was I that in the vanity of my heart put such notions in thy head. It was I that tempted thee."

"It was the duyvel," muttered St. Nicholas, "in the shape of a pretty wife."

Johannes gave his helpmate a look of affectionate forgiveness, and went on to tell St. Nicholas how, finally egged on by the evil example of his neighbours, he had at last committed sacrilege against his household gods, and pulled down the home of his fathers, commencing a new one on its ruins.

"Donderdag!" quoth the saint to himself; "and the bricks came from faderland too!"

When Johannes had about half finished his new house, he discovered one day, to his great astonishment and dismay, that all his money, which he had been saving for his children, was gone. His strong box was empty, and his house but half finished, although, after estimating the cost, he had allowed one third more in order to be sure in the business.

Johannes was now at a dead stand. The idea of borrowing money and running in debt never entered his head before, and probably would not now, had it not been suggested to him by a neighbour, a great speculator, who had lately built a whole street of houses, not a single brick of which belonged to him in reality. He had borrowed the money, mortgaged the property, and expected to grow rich by a sudden rise. Poor Johannes may be excused for listening to the seductions of this losel varlet, seeing he had a house half finished on his hands; but whether so or not, he did listen and was betrayed into borrowing money of a bank just then established in the *Colonie* on a capital paid in according to law—that is, not paid at all—the directors of which were very anxious to exchange their rags for lands and houses.

Johannes finished his house in glorious style, and having opened this new mine of wealth, furnished it still more gloriously; and as it would have been sheer nonsense not to live gloriously in such a glorious establishment, spent thrice his income in order to

keep up his respectability. He was going on swim-
mingly, when what is called a reaction took place;
which means, as far as I can understand, that the
bank directors, having been pleased to make money
plenty to increase their dividends, are pleased thereafter to make it scarce for the same purpose. Instead
of lending it in the name of the bank, it is credibly
reported they do it through certain brokers, who
charge lawful interest and unlawful commission, and
thus cheat the law with a clear conscience. But I
thank Heaven devoutly that I know nothing of their
wicked mysteries, and therefore will say no more
about them.

Be this as it may, Johannes was called upon all of
a sudden to pay his notes to the bank, for the reaction
had commenced, and there were no more renewals.
The directors wanted all the money to lend out at
three per cent a month. It became necessary to raise
the wind, as they say in Wall-street, and Johannes,
by the advice of his good friend the speculative genius, went with him to a certain money lender of his
acquaintance, who was reckoned a good Christian
because he always charged most usury where there
was the greatest necessity for a loan. To a rich man
he would lend at something like a reasonable interest, but to a man in great distress for money he

showed about as much mercy as a weazel does to a chicken. He sucked their blood till there was not a drop left in their bodies. This he did six days in the week, and on the seventh went three times to church, to enable him to begin the next week with a clear conscience. Beshrew such varlets, I say; they bring religion itself into disrepute, and add the sin of hypocrisy to men to that of insult to Heaven.

Suffice it to say, that poor Johannes Garrebrantze the younger went down hill faster than he ever went up in his life; and inasmuch as I scorn these details of petty roguery as unworthy of my cloth and calling, I shall content myself with merely premising that by a process very common nowadays, the poor man was speedily bereft of all the patrimony left him by his worthy father in paying commission to the money lender. He finally became bankrupt; and inasmuch as he was unacquainted with the mystery of getting rich by such a manoeuvre, was left without a shilling in the world. He retired from his fine house, which was forthwith occupied by his good friend the money lender, whose nose had been tweaked by St. Nicholas, as heretofore recorded, and took refuge in the wretched building where he was found by that benevolent worthy. Destitute of resources, and entirely unacquainted with the art of living by his wits or his labours, though he tried hard both ways, poor Johannes became gradually steeped in poverty to the very lips, and being totally disabled by rheumatism, might, peradventure, with all his family, have perished that very night, had not Providence mercifully sent the good St. Nicholas to their relief.

"Wat donderdag!" exclaimed the saint, when he had done—*"wat donderdag!"*—was that your house down yonder, with the fine bedroom, the wardrobes, the looking-glass as big as the moon, and the bedstead with a cocked hat and feathers?"

"Even so," replied the other, hanging down his head.

"Is het mogelyk!" And after considering a little while, the good saint slapped his hand on the table, broke forth again—"By donderdag, but I'll soon settle this business."

He then began to hum an old Dutch hymn, which by its soothing and wholesome monotony so operated upon Johannes and his family that one and all fell fast asleep in their chairs.

The good St. Nicholas then lighted his pipe, and seating himself by the fire, revolved in his mind the best mode of proceeding on this occasion. At first he determined to divest the rich money lender of all his ill-gotten gains, and bestow them on poor Johannes and his family. But when he considered that the losel caitiff was already sufficiently punished in being condemned to the sordid toils of money making, and in the privation of all those social and benevolent feelings which, while they contribute to our own happiness, administer to that of others; that he was for ever beset with the consuming cares of avarice, the hope of gain, and the fear of losses; and that, rich as he was, he suffered all the gnawing pangs of an insatiable desire for more—when he considered all this, St. Nicholas decided to leave him to the certain punishment of ill-gotten wealth, and the chances of losing it by an over craving appetite for its increase, which sooner or later produces all the consequences of reckless imprudence.

"Let the splutterkin alone," thought St. Nicholas, "and he will become the instrument of his own punishment."

Then he went on to think what he should do for poor Johannes and his little children. Though he had been severely punished for his folly, yet did the good saint, who in his nightly holyday peregrinations had seen more of human life and human passions than the sun ever shone upon, very well know that sudden wealth, or sudden poverty, is a sore trial of the heart of man, in like manner as the sudden transition from

light to darkness, or darkness to light, produces a
temporary blindness. It was true that Johannes had
received a severe lesson, but the great mass of mankind are prone to forget the chastening rod of experience, as they do the pangs of sickness when they are
past. He therefore settled in his mind that the return
of Johannes to competence and prosperity should be
by the salutary process of his own exertions, and that
he should learn their value by the pains it cost to
attain them. *"Het is goed visschen in troebel water,"*
quoth he, "for then a man knows the value of what
he catches."

It was broad daylight before he had finished his
pipe and his cogitations, and placing his old polished
delft pipe carefully in his buttonhole, the good saint
sallied forth, leaving Johannes and his family still fast
asleep in their chairs. Directly opposite the miserable
abode of Johannes there dwelt a little fat Dutchman,
of a reasonable competency, who had all his life man-
fully stemmed the torrent of modern innovation. He
eschewed all sorts of paper money as an invention of
people without property to get hold of those that
had it; abhorred the practice of widening streets; and
despised in his heart all public improvements except
canals, a sneaking notion for which he inherited from
old faderland. He was honest as the light of the

blessed sun; and though he opened his best parlour but twice a year to have it cleaned and put to rights, yet this I will say of him, that the poor man who wanted a dinner was never turned away from his table. The worthy burgher was standing at the street door, which opened in the middle, and leaning over the lower half, so that the smoke of his pipe ascended in the clear frosty morning in a little white column far into the sky before it was dissipated.

St. Nicholas stopped his wagon right before his door, and cried out in a clear hearty voice,

"Good-morning, good-morning, mynheer; and a happy Newyear to you."

"Good-morning," cried the hale old burgher, "and many happy Newyears to *you.* Hast got any good fat hen turkies to sell?" for he took him for a countryman coming in to market. St. Nicholas answered and said that he had been on a different errand that morning; and the other cordially invited him to alight, come in, and take a glass of hot spiced rum, with the which it was his custom to regale all comers at the jolly Newyear. The invitation was frankly accepted, for the worthy St. Nicholas, though no toper, was never a member of the temperance society. He chose to be keeper of his own conscience, and was of opinion that a man who is obliged to sign an obligation not to drink, will be very likely to break it the first convenient opportunity.

As they sat cozily together, by a rousing fire of wholesome and enlivening hickory, the little plump Dutchman occasionally inveighing stoutly against paper money, railroads, improving streets, and the like, the compassionate saint took occasion to utter a wish that the poor man over the way and his starving family had some of the good things that were so rife on Newyear's day, for he had occasion to know that they were suffering all the evils of the most abject poverty.

"The splutterkin," exclaimed the little fat burgher—"he is as proud as Lucifer himself. I had a suspicion of this, and sought divers occasions to get acquainted with him, that I might have some excuse for prying into his necessities, and take the privilege of an old neighbour to relieve them. But *vuur en vlammen!* would you believe it—he avoided me just as if he owed me money, and couldn't pay."

St. Nicholas observed that if it was ever excusable for a man to be proud, it was when he fell into a state where every one, high and low, worthless and honourable, looked down upon him with contempt. Then he related to him the story of poor Johannes, and taking from his pocket a heavy purse, he offered it to the worthy old burgher, who swore he would be dondered if he wanted any of his money.

"But hearken to me," said the saint; "yon foolish lad is the son of an old friend of mine, who did me many a kindness in his day, for which I am willing to requite his posterity. Thou shalt take this purse and bestow a small portion of it, as from thyself, as a loan from time to time, as thou seest he deserves it by his exertions. It may happen, as I hope it will, that in good time he will acquire again the competency he hath lost by his own folly and inexperience; and as he began the world a worthy, respectable citizen, I beseech thee to do this—to be his friend, and to watch over him and his little ones, in the name of St. Nicholas."

The portly burgher promised that he would, and they parted with marvellous civility, St. Nicholas having promised to visit him again should his life be spared. He then mounted his little wagon, and the little Dutchman having turned his head for an instant, when he looked again could see nothing of the saint or his equipage. *"Is het mogelyk!"* exclaimed he, and his mind misgave him that there was something unaccountable in the matter.

My story is already too long, peradventure, else

would I describe the astonishment of Johannes and his wife when they awoke and found the benevolent stranger had departed without bidding them farewell. They would have thought all that had passed was but a dream, had not the fragments of the good things on which they regaled during the night borne testimony to its reality. Neither will I detail how, step by step, aided by the advice and countenance of the worthy little Dutchman, and the judicious manner of his dispensing the bounty of St. Nicholas, Johannes Garrebrantze, by a course of industry, economy, and integrity, at length attained once again the station he had lost by his follies and extravagance. Suffice it to say that though he practised a rational self-denial in all his outlayings, he neither became a miser, nor did he value money except as the means of obtaining the comforts of life, and administering to the happiness of others.

In the mean time, the money lender, not being content with the wealth he had obtained by taking undue advantage of the distresses of others, and becoming every day more greedy, launched out into mighty speculations. He founded a score of towns without any houses in them; dealt by hundreds of thousands in fancy stocks; and finally became the victim of one of his own speculations, by in time coming to believe in the very deceptions he had practised upon others. It is an old saying, that the greatest rogue in the world, sooner or later, meets with his match, and so it happened with the money lender. He was seduced into the purchase of a town without any houses in it, at an expense of millions; was met by one of those reactions that play the mischief with honest labourers, and thus finally perished in a bottomless pit of his own digging. Finding himself sinking, he resorted to forgeries, and had by this means raised money to such an amount that his villainy almost approached to sublimity. His property, as the phrase is, came under the hammer, and Johannes purchased his own house at half the price it cost him in building.

The good St. Nicholas trembled at the new ordeal to which Johannes had subjected himself; but finding, when he visited him, as he did regularly every Newyear's eve, that he was cured of his foolish vanities, and that his wife was one of the best housekeepers in all Fort Orange, he discarded his apprehensions, and rejoiced in the prosperity that was borne so meekly and wisely. The little fat Dutchman lived a long time in expectation that the stranger in the one-horse wagon would come for the payment of his purse of money; but finding that year after year rolled away without his appearing, often said to himself, as he sat on his stoop with a pipe in his mouth,

"I'll be dondered if I don't believe it was the good St. Nicholas."

New York Classics, *a series devoted to reprinting regional literature of lasting value.*

Frank Bergmann, *Series Editor*